A TURBULENT PRIEST

A TURBULENT PRIEST

J.M. Gregson

This first world edition published in Great Britain 2000 by
SEVERN HOUSE PUBLISHERS LTD of
9–15 High Street, Sutton, Surrey SM1 1DF.
This first world edition published in the U.S.A. 2000 by
SEVERN HOUSE PUBLISHERS INC of
595 Madison Avenue, New York, N.Y. 10022.

British Library Cataloguing in Publication Data

Gregson,   J. M. (James Michael)

A turbulent priest
1.Peach, Detective Inspector (Fictitious character) – Fiction
2.Blake, Detective Sergeant (Fictitious character) – Fiction
3.Police – England – Lancashire – Fiction
4.Detective and mystery stories

I. Title
823.9'14 [F]

ISBN 0-7278-5519-0

Typeset by Palimpsest Book Production Ltd.,
Polmont, Stirlingshire, Scotland.
Printed and bound in Great Britain by
MPG Books Ltd, Bodmin, Cornwall.

To Rose, who reads, reasons, reduces, remonstrates and never reproaches

"Will no one rid me of this turbulent priest?"
Henry II, speaking of Thomas Beckett

One

It never stopped raining on that fateful Monday. Even allowing for the fact that this was a Bank Holiday in England, the downpour was exceptional.

On the Lancashire coast, which often escaped the worst of the weather as the clouds drifted towards the Pennines forty miles inland, the rain fell in sheets over a grey and sullen sea. In Morecambe and Blackpool and Southport, the holiday crowds and the day-trippers wandered damply along the promenades, stared resentfully at the low banks of emptying cloud, and turned hopelessly to the packed amusement arcades and the few remaining cinemas to find what shelter they could. On this miserable last day of August, Blackpool's famous Tower absorbed thousands of these unfortunates, but its topmost point remained blanketed in cloud throughout the day.

Things were scarcely better inland, as the clouds moved on the slightest of breezes towards those invisible Pennine heights. While those sensible Lancashire folk who had decided to keep off the crowded Bank Holiday roads congratulated themselves grimly upon their wisdom, the rain fell even more heavily thirty miles inland than on the coast. Detective Inspector Percy Peach gazed miserably out of the window of the North Lancs Golf Club at the pools of water which grew ever wider upon the eighteenth green outside, cursed the weather, and ordered another pint. At one o'clock, even he and his equally determined companions had to accept that there would be no golf on that sodden day.

Further up the valleys of the Ribble and the Hodder, in the hills where these picturesque waterways had their sources, it rained even harder. There was no thunder, but the moisture fell with cloudburst intensity, not for ten minutes, as it might have done in a thunderstorm, but for hour after hour. The streams which had been at their summer lows after five weeks of drought stirred into life. Water which had been almost stagnant became by noon a steady trickle, by two o'clock a brown tumble of noise. By five, most of the country roads were impassable because of floods, and the water in streams and rivers was roaring towards the coast and the sea in angry torrents.

The floods dislodged things which had lain unmoving through the languid weeks of summer heat. The rubbish left by an untidy society was gathered from where it had been tossed. From culverts and from ditches, from the banks of streams and rivers, packaging from food, empty plastic bottles, and other, less savoury items were dislodged, lifted and borne swiftly away by the rising waters. Towards the end of the day, logs, even the occasional whole tree with its roots turning crazily in the brown flood, passed swiftly down the Ribble and its tributaries, awesome flotsam for those few hardy souls who could bear to stand and observe on the bridges in the unrelenting downpour.

Almost five centimetres of rain had fallen in parts of the Ribble Valley in the last twenty-four hours, said Radio Lancashire at six o'clock. Or two inches, the announcer added thoughtfully for his older listeners. A hell of a lot anyway, said his sidekick, in the chatty style which was now considered obligatory for local radio. DI Peach, returning home from the golf club to find the test match washed out, swore at the cheerful girl and feinted to kick the set.

And still it rained, as the light diminished quickly on this gloomiest of evenings. Ditches which for the rest of the year were no more than field-drains became temporary streams, as the waters filled them and rose high enough to seek a way out of these narrow trenches. Things were lifted and moved which might have remained undiscovered for months, even years, without this extraordinary and relentless opening of the heavens. Curious things, like scarcely-worn wellingtons. Amusing things, like a portrait of Adolf Hitler, still in its wooden frame but with the marks of darts all round the face and 'Fuck the Führer' inscribed as a motto by some alliterative genius of half a century earlier.

And there was more disquieting detritus also, though no one saw the first movements of the most ominous of all. It lay beneath the brambles which scrambled across the top of the ditch, covered in twigs and the dead leaves of former autumns. It was heavy, and it remained static through the first six hours of the deluge, whilst the water rose around it, dislodged its covering and floated that noiselessly away. It was six o'clock before the insistent rising of the water caused this heaviest of flotsam to lift from the bottom of the ditch. It was seven o'clock before the water brimmed against the very top of the ditch and the thing floated free and slowly moved upon the surface.

And still the rain drummed relentlessly, on the back of what had once been a living human head. There was no living person yet to observe its progress, but the corpse inched sluggishly along the edge of the wood which the ditch skirted towards the rushing waters of the stream fifty yards away.

By eight o'clock, the carcass was moving swiftly down the brown torrent of the racing stream towards the swollen Ribble, scarcely a mile away. The rain fell still – would go on, indeed, without abatement until after midnight on that sodden Monday. The corpse might easily have reached the river and been carried swiftly away to sea and oblivion on the flood, had it not been for the willpower of a young Labrador.

The animal was determined to enjoy its normal evening walk and could not understand the reluctance of its master to relish the refreshment of a little rain upon his face. At eight o'clock, the dog prevailed and leapt joyfully into the near-darkness of this dismal day. His owner followed reluctantly, oilskinned to his very eyebrows, hunched against the downpour, cursing his canine charge, resentful of the obvious joy exhibited in the dog's every bounding movement. With his left hand thrust deep into his pocket and his right hand gripping the walking stick he carried to control the dog, the man trudged out to inspect the bridge over the stream at the edge of the village, a macabre curiosity driving him to see just how high the waters had risen against its ancient stones on this, the wettest day he could recall.

The water was almost touching the topmost point of the arch itself, its sound roaring as he had never heard it before, scarcely two feet beneath him as he stood upon the bridge, the vibrations strong enough to prevent him lingering in contemplation of the racing flood below him. As he moved away, he caught sight of something that set his pulse racing. It poked out from the driftwood which had gathered where the waters eddied at the edge of the bank near the bridge. It was the back of a human hand, grey-white against the brown of the raging waters.

He was reluctant to believe the evidence of his eyes in the little light that was left but, as he watched, he saw shoulders, then the back of a head – almost submerged, but lifting and falling unmistakably with the movement of the current on the edge of this miniature maelstrom. The body lifted, moved in a half-circle, threatened to join the mainstream again and be borne away beneath the bridge. For an instant the hand rose almost clear of the waters, as if in mute supplication against the indignity of its helplessness.

The man scrambled to the edge of the water, hooked the handle of his walking-stick beneath the collar and the hair of the corpse, and pulled it carefully to the sand and stones of the bank. He hauled it heavily on to the sodden grass, where it would be safe from the torrent. He yelled at the excited dog when it began to bark, made it obey him and keep away from the body. But he could not control his own breathing, which came in great, uneven gasps. He did not know whether it was the effort or the revulsion which made him gasp like this.

He was careful not to turn the body over. He did not want to see the face, nor any part of it.

It should have been easy to tap out the digits of 999, but he found it needed all his concentration to control fingers which seemed to be no longer at his command. When a calm voice answered, "Emergency: which service, please?" his own voice sounded both hoarse and high-pitched in his ears, like that of an over-excited stranger. He had to concentrate hard to give the details of his find and his position. An ambulance and a police vehicle would be there very quickly, he was told. He nodded dumbly at the instrument, unable to speak at all now that the essentials of his news had been delivered.

By nine o'clock, Detective Inspector Peach knew that this Bank Holiday was not after all to conclude in the boredom and frustration which had characterised the rest of it for him. There was work to do. A suspicious death.

Two

B y seven thirty on the morning after the great deluge of 31st August, it was fine. There was even a wan sun to illuminate the dripping scene. But it was cool enough to make DI Peach feel that autumn was not too far away as he got out of his car beside the swollen stream.

Plastic tapes had been hastily strung round the area where the corpse lay during the previous evening's downpour. They hung motionless in the still, damp air. The hollow-eyed young constable who had maintained a lonely vigil here throughout the night had been relieved now, but he lingered at the edge of the scene for a moment, hoping for a word of praise or recognition from the officer who was in charge of the case. Percy grinned cheerfully into the exhausted young face. "Just what you joined for, eh lad? Whole night to yourself without any interference from the station sergeant! Nice little skive for you, that!"

"Well, sir, it wasn't exactly—"

"On overtime too, I expect. Got it made, some of you lads have." He glanced at the little cube of canvas erected over the corpse. "Didn't say anything to you during the night, did he? Like who he was, or how he got here?" The young constable trudged stiffly to his car, taking care not to mutter "Cocky CID bastard!" until he was out of sight and earshot.

6

Peach nodded affably to the sergeant in charge of the Scene of Crime team. "Police surgeon been and gone, has he?" However dead a corpse might be, however long ago it had perished, death had still to be officially confirmed by a doctor. Mere policemen would not suffice.

"Yes. Been dead for some time, he said. At least a week, he thought. The meat wagon and the men with the body bag will be here soon; they've had to wait until they could get a pathologist to come out with them to supervise the removal. We shan't find much here, you know. Patently obvious the poor bugger didn't die where he was found." Joe Jackson, a grizzled officer now looking forward to his retirement, always took it personally when his work was difficult. He glared malevolently at the little tent, as if it was inconsiderate of the man inside it to have left the world so unhelpfully.

Percy went and drew back the flap of the tent. Apprehensively, because this was not a new corpse. But the water had removed the worst of the smells; Percy ducked and moved his squat body cautiously over the remains of what had recently been a man. The corpse lay face down, as it had been found. The backs of the hands were bloated and white, looking too big for the thin arms, like hands in a child's drawing. There was no sign of a ring, nor any sign that the swollen fingers had ever carried one. But that didn't mean the man hadn't been married: not all married men wore rings, despite what Percy considered the deplorable modern tendency to do so.

Peach stooped and lifted the right hand gingerly with his pen. Soft, unmarked white flesh. No signs of abrasions or calluses. Difficult to be certain after the effects of the water, but he'd guess this man hadn't been a manual worker. Percy didn't look at the face, which lay completely invisible amidst the lush wet grass. He knew what happened with an older

7

corpse. The eyes went first, usually, if there were birds around. And various bugs he preferred not to itemise got into the mouth and began their work. He felt no pressing urge to look at the face.

It was only when the 'death wagon' rolled to a halt beside the bridge and the men climbed carefully down the slope with the plastic shell to take away the body that Joe Jackson reluctantly volunteered his single useful piece of information. "Police surgeon did say one thing, Percy. This poor bugger didn't die from drowning. He didn't think he'd been in the water very long."

Percy Peach rapped hard on the door inscribed 'Detective Superintendent Tucker, Head of CID Section', causing the room's occupant to spill his coffee over the digestive biscuit in his saucer.

"Sorry to bother you, sir," he said cheerfully to the man behind the big desk, "but I wonder if you have any insights that you're able to pass on yet about this suspicious death out beyond Clitheroe."

Percy knew perfectly well that Tucker had only just arrived in the building: he had watched through his window as the Super had climbed stiffly out of his Rover in the car park. But Peach's twin missions in life were to make life difficult for criminals and to make life hell for his chief, the man he called Tommy Bloody Tucker. These missions gave him equal satisfaction, but he found baiting Tucker much the easier of the two. In Percy's opinion, Tucker had reached his exalted position by shameless creeping and skilful appropriation of credit which should have gone to others; thus he deserved to be kept hopping about a bit as he sought a quiet life and waited for his fat pension. Tucker wouldn't even know yet about the case for which he would be nominally responsible.

The Superintendent looked suspiciously at Peach as he poured the coffee back into his cup. "I haven't had time to catch up on that yet. You've no idea of the mountain of administration that was waiting for me this morning, you know."

"Indeed I haven't, sir, thank goodness. But I know you relieve us of hours of paperwork by your enlightened managerial practices – I often tell the lads that. They don't all understand, of course, but they don't see you operating at close quarters, as I have the privilege of doing."

Tucker wondered for the hundredth time how he could deny this close quarters contact to Peach, without finding a solution. The man seemed positively to enjoy having work piled upon his shoulders. And when his chief had pulled off what he thought a masterstroke, and given Peach a young female Detective Sergeant to contend with, the man had taken it in his stride like everything else. Tucker said gloomily, "You'd better enlighten me, Percy."

Peach thought that there wasn't a man on this earth who could do that. "I'll put you in the picture, yes, sir." He wondered whether to adopt the tone of a constable reading from his notebook in court for his report, then decided this would be going too far: rank had some dangers, even when it was carried by men like Tucker. "Thanks to your shouldering the burdens of administration, I was able to get out to Bolton-by-Bowland at half-past seven this morning. The police surgeon had already certified death – the chap was found late last night, sir, I believe."

"Chap?" Tucker's dull repetition of the word was due to the fact that he had made the mistake of picking up his

9

sodden digestive biscuit from his saucer. It fell on to his tie, then slid like a brown slug on to his immaculate white shirt, which it continued to descend like a snail in slow motion through the rest of their conversation. Tucker tried to ignore it; Peach's eyes widened unblinkingly as they followed its progress, whilst his heart sang within him.

"Male Caucasian IC One, sir. Found dead beside a stream in flood just outside Bolton-by-Bowland. Now on his way to the Home Office Forensic Science Laboratory at Chorley."

Tucker should have known about this. He wondered who to blame. But his phone had been off the hook at his wife's insistence last night, whilst they entertained her parents and an aunt. Peach seemed to know these things, to be able always to pierce the easy lies he got away with for the rest of his day. It would be safer just to minimise this, to take the wind out of his sententious Inspector's sails. Tucker looked at his immaculate nails, trying to ignore the creeping mess on the front of his shirt. "Just a vagrant, I expect. Someone who'd been living rough."

Percy looked puzzled. "Interesting thought, sir. I thought perhaps a white-collar worker of some kind. I inspected the hands, you see, and they didn't look like a manual worker's, or a vagrant's."

"Ah, you must beware of jumping to conclusions, Peach. All good detectives should beware of generalisations made on too little evidence."

That was rich, coming from a man who thought any rural death must be that of a vagrant, thought Percy. "Yes, sir. I'll try to remember that. I think you may have reminded me of it before, but I have such a terrible memory for these things."

Tucker glared at the round, earnest face with its black toothbrush moustache beneath the prematurely bald head. As usual with this Inspector who looked like a smaller Oliver Hardy, he thought he was being mocked, but could not put his finger on the precise phrase. "Yes. Anyway, if it's not a vagrant, I expect it's a routine domestic death. Manslaughter maybe, rather than murder. Four fifths of killings take place within the family, you know."

Percy did. Every policeman did. It was one of the first things they were told in training. He could even have brought Tucker's statistics up to date, given him a percentage for the last recorded year. Instead, he said, "Yes, that's very useful to know, sir. Might be worth your setting your thoughts down on paper and circulating them more widely. Of course, in this case, we don't yet know that there's been any killing. Might be a suicide. Might even be natural causes. No doubt the forensic wizards will tell us, in due course."

Tucker was furious with himself. He should have said that at the outset, demoting this death, pretending he would only show interest if it emerged that there was real meat for a top CID man like him to feed on. It was too late now. He snarled, "Well. What else do we know?"

"Not a lot, sir, as yet. Doctor Martin wouldn't venture much, as usual, but he did say that he thought the man had been dead for some time. More than a week, he thought. We've checked the missing persons register, but not come up with anyone. Looks at the moment as though he wasn't reported missing."

Tucker decided that the only thing to do was to stick to his guns. "Sounds to me like a suspicious death, you know." He brightened at the thought of difficulties ahead for his tormentor. "If it is a murder, it won't be easy to find the killer, you know, after this much time has elapsed. Sixty per cent of killings which are not detected in the first week remain unsolved, you know. You've already missed the most vital time for investigation."

He smiled blandly at Peach. Not only had he come out with another generalisation which every copper and most of the public knew, thought Percy, but he seemed positively pleased at the thought that it was going to be difficult for his staff. "That is true, sir. The team may need the full benefit of your expertise and experience to succeed on this one." He watched his chief's face cloud with dismay, then switched his ground again. "Though as I say, we don't know yet that this is a murder. At present, we have only an unidentified corpse. Could be an accidental death or a suicide. As good detectives, we must beware of generalisations made on too little evidence."

This time, Tucker knew it was insolence: to have his own words quoted back to him like this was plainly insubordinate. But it was difficult to know what to do about it, with Peach's round, expressionless gaze fixed firmly at some point above his victim's head. Tucker said desperately, "Well, anyway, we'll see what forensic can tell us about this drowning. They often come up with—"

"Not a drowning, sir." This time Percy denied himself any reiteration of Tucker's injunctions about generalisations. Instead, he transferred his gaze back to the superintendent's face and allowed himself the most childishly innocent of his range of smiles. "That was the one useful thing our police surgeon volunteered, apparently. Chummy was dead before he went into the water."

Tucker felt his mind reeling. An appropriate word, for a man floundering like a fish on a line. He said tentatively, "Then it looks as if our man might have been killed by someone else after all."

12

"Oh, I should think that's very likely, sir. I didn't want to jump to any unwarranted conclusions. But I did notice a bloody great gash across the back of his head."

"There's no need for this, you know," said DI Peach. Chivalry did not come easily to him, especially when he found it rejected.

Detective Sergeant Lucy Blake smiled and snatched a sideways glance at him as she drove. She liked him when he was an old chauvinist softy, though she couldn't possibly let him know it. "I wouldn't miss it for the world. Part of the learning process, a post mortem is, as you said when you insisted on my attending the first one. Seems a long time ago now."

She was secretly relieved to find that the post mortem was complete by the time they drove into the quiet grounds of the forensic laboratory at Chorley. She would have tightened the muscles of her stomach as usual if she had needed to stand by during the cutting of the corpse and the investigation of its organs, but she preferred not to have her digestion tested in this way, despite her assurances to Percy Peach.

The Home Office pathologist was brisk and breezy; in her limited experience practitioners of this grisly calling often were. "Looks as though you have a murder to investigate," he said cheerfully, as he peeled off his gloves and unhooked the microphone into which he had dictated his findings whilst he worked. "My name's Browne. You'll have my full report by tomorrow. If it's any help, I'll give you my thoughts on the major findings right now."

"Thank you. The less time we waste the better, when a man's already been dead for several days." Peach was also aware that a man submitting a report which might eventually

13

be probed in court by a defence counsel had to be cautious on paper; no one liked being made to look a fool in public, and least of all a fool in his profession. It meant that PM reports confined themselves to facts, when a little informed speculation might well be more useful to the officers beginning an investigation.

"Right you are." Browne led them into an office dominated by a huge desk, which was littered with letters and documents, very unlike the neat precision of the stainless steel counters and sinks he had left behind him. He gestured at two chairs; they had to remove cardboard boxes from them before they could sit. He slumped opposite them and took off his green cap, leaving his thinning grey hair in disarray, but kept on the green rubber gumboots he wore in the lab as he slumped down in an armchair opposite them. They had been well washed, but there was a small smear of brown blood on his left sleeve, reminding them through his cheerful demeanour of what he had been doing whilst they drove here from Brunton.

"He was dead before he ever went into the water," said Browne.

Percy did not say they knew that: these people worked better if they thought they were giving you lots of new information. Instead, he raised his eyebrows and said, "How did he die?"

The man opposite them drew a deep breath, waved his arms in the air a little, then changed his mind. "Come into the lab and I'll show you. My report is full of 'might haves' and 'in all probabilities', but I think I can show you what happened." He led the way briskly back whence he had come. Good, thought Percy, an enthusiast. You always got more out of enthusiasts.

Browne drew back the sheet from the head Peach had seen by the stream nine hours earlier. For the first time, he saw the face he had then chosen to leave in decent oblivion. The pathologist, or more likely his assistant, had made a neat job of stitching up the incision made from ear to ear over the top of the head for the post mortem. Someone would still have to identify what was left of this fellow, when they had found out who he was. Peach didn't envy that person the task.

The eyes were damaged, as he had thought they might be: what was left of the eyelids had been pulled down over the empty sockets. The pathologist lifted the shoulders stiffly sideways before they could dwell upon what creatures had been busy around the mouth. "This chap was given a hell of a clout across the back of his head." With a silver ball-point, he indicated the white, bloodless scar which Percy had seen in the dark hair earlier. The hair had been shaved away now, to expose the trenching. "Various insect damage to the flesh around the scar, which we should ignore for our purposes. No blood left, owing to the cleansing of last night's flood. Unfortunately, no wood fibres or other evidence as to what he might have been hit with, for the same reason. The traditional blunt instrument; I'm afraid I can't say more."

"Did that kill him?"

"In my opinion, no. It was a hefty blow, enough to render a man insensible, or certainly so dazed that he would not be able to defend himself. But the actual cause of death was almost certainly vagal inhibition – strangulation, if you prefer the layman's term." The silver pen moved to the carotid artery in the neck and hovered briefly over the line of a livid crimson-black line around the unnaturally white flesh. Lucy Blake tried to ignore the stitching she could see in the middle of the neck, which she knew was the top point of an incision running from the mark she could see to the pubis

15

beneath the sheet; the cut made to enable the pathologist to remove the chest and abdominal organs en masse. Much better to concentrate on what this breezy, experienced fifty-year-old had to tell them. "This was probably made by a thin nylon rope or a length of wire. Again the water has removed any traces which might have clung to the skin, I'm afraid. But this is what dispatched your man from the land of the living."

"Could a woman have killed him?"

"Certainly. The blow to the back of the head could have been delivered by a woman, or even a child, with the right implement and the right leverage. After that, he was killed by some sort of ligature round the neck, as you can see. No great strength required for that, especially if he was unconscious or nearly unconscious at the time."

"You don't think he was able to put up much of a fight?"

"No, I don't. He was probably in his forties and reasonably fit, despite a bit of a paunch. Five feet nine and eleven stone eight. But there is no bruising on his hands and arms, and nothing under the nails that would indicate a struggle – you'll see from my report that I don't think he was in the water long enough for all such traces to be removed. My guess is that he was hit from behind, then dispatched at leisure. Probably never given a chance to defend himself."

"How long had he been in the water?"

Browne pursed his lips. "My report will say not more than a day, and that's what I'd have to stick to in court. Probably it was considerably less than that. There are none of the symptoms of prolonged immersion: no 'washerwoman's skin' or damage by river creatures. There is hypostasis throughout the body, indicating that the corpse has been lying prone on its back for a considerable period. The blood has settled noticeably into the lower back, buttocks and thighs."

Browne glanced surreptitiously at DS Blake, found her cheeks still reassuringly peach rather than white. "There are certain other areas of damage in the corpse which could only have been achieved whilst it was above ground, I'm afraid. The maggots have been at work. Busy little chaps, maggots; informative, too, in this context. I have passed relevant specimens to our forensic entomologist, although I have a certain amount of expertise in this field myself. As you are probably aware, the degree of development of grubs found within the corpse often enables us to be fix a time of death with reasonable precision."

"So when do you think our Mr X died?"

"You'll have to wait for the expert's opinion to confirm that. My report says between one and two weeks, but I'd say from the maggots ten to twelve days. Allowing for the hot weather which preceded yesterday's downpour."

"You can be that precise?" said Lucy Blake.

"The experts can. And I think our expert will confirm my opinion in the next twenty-four hours." Browne spoke with modest pride, like a birdwatcher confident of a sighting. "We couldn't swear to it in court, of course, but if you want a starting point for your enquiries, I would suggest ten to twelve days ago for the time of death."

"All right," said Peach. "You've told us how he died. You've given us a reasonable idea when. What about where?"

"That we can't help you with, I'm afraid. You'll have to search for possible sites and send any materials from them to forensic. We've sent his clothes for analysis, of course; sports coat and trousers, shirt, jockey shorts, short summer socks, quite good leather shoes. But I don't think you'll get much from any of them: the water will have removed most things which might have been helpful."

Peach nodded gloomily. There was nothing they could do about it, but when the Press began to bleat about police bafflement, they wouldn't trouble to report the difficulties they faced. "So he was strangled, not drowned. Presumably someone dumped him in the stream?"

"That would be the normal assumption. This is CID territory rather than pathology, but it seems unlikely to me. If you wanted to dispose of a body, you'd dump it in a major river, like the Ribble or the Hodder, wouldn't you? Somewhere where it might be swiftly carried away, hopefully out to sea – not a village stream where it might be found quite quickly. And wouldn't you do it as soon as you'd killed your victim? As I say, this chap wasn't in the water for very long. It's unlikely that anyone would have kept a body for ten days and then slung it into the river, isn't it?"

"Yes." I should have said all that, thought Peach. Still, Browne had been helpful, interested in their problems rather than dourly official. "It's conceivable, of course, that someone had to wait his opportunity to dispose of the corpse, and saw yesterday's floods as his chance. We'll have to bear that possibility in mind, until we can prove otherwise, but it's not the most likely scenario, I agree." That was a phrase Tommy Bloody Tucker might have produced, he thought; he'd better watch himself. He looked down at the shape beneath them. Browne had drawn the sheet back over the head, emphasising the anonymity of death. "Our first problem is going to be finding who the poor bugger is. No one's reported him missing."

"And I fancy whoever killed him didn't intend to make it easy for you. We'll make a cast of the jaws in the next hour or so. The dental records should show you who he is, if no one comes forward to claim him once you break the news of the death."

Peach nodded, feeling despite himself the familiar rise in excitement at the thought of pitting his wits against an enemy as yet unknown. "Anything useful in the pockets?"

Browne smiled grimly. "That's what I meant when I said your killer wasn't making it easy. The pockets have been totally emptied."

Three

"The body of a man was found near the village of Bolton-by-Bowland last night. Police say that the corpse, which was discovered in a swollen brook at the climax of yesterday's Bank Holiday deluge, is that of a man of about forty years of age. They are treating the death as suspicious. The body has not yet been identified, and anyone who thinks he or she might be able to help in this matter is asked to contact CID headquarters at Brunton Police Station."

The announcement came in the Radio Lancashire news bulletin at midday. The murderer heard it only by chance.

It was a chilling moment, fixing the words which had seemed only half-heard vividly in the mind, so that they chimed through the next hour like a clock striking its quarters. The spot mentioned in the radio announcement wasn't where the corpse had been laid: the image of that prone form, carefully hidden between twigs and brambles in the ditch which had seemed so remote, reared itself vividly before the killer's eyes, as it had done so often in the last ten days. But that ditch wasn't far from Bolton-by-Bowland. And surely there couldn't be two corpses lying so close to each other in such a quiet, rural place?

At first, it seemed there would be nothing on the one o'clock television news. Then, halfway through the local news on

Granada, it came. There was a picture of the spot where the corpse had been found, with the brook still in swirling spate around the arches of the stone bridge and police tapes which cordoned the place hanging limply in the background. Only two pieces of information were added to the official handout which the local radio had carried an hour earlier. The first was unimportant: the body had been discovered by a man taking his dog for its evening walk at the height of the evening downpour. The second set the murderer's pulses tingling: police believed that the corpse had been carried to the point of its discovery by the quite exceptional deluge. Much of the surrounding area was under flood waters which were now beginning to subside, and the members of the police team already assembled were now searching for the spot where the body had originally lain.

There was a brief sequence from a hand-held camera of a line of policemen in wellingtons moving in formation along the side of a wood, and the killer knew immediately from the numbers employed that this was being treated as a murder hunt.

The person who was to be the quarry in this search turned off the television as the announcer switched to sport. Quiet, absolute quiet, seemed suddenly necessary. You had to think coolly to keep things clear, and that seemed difficult with the shock of this revelation still throbbing in your head. It was bad luck that the corpse had been discovered like this, so soon. Just as a result of weather no one could have foreseen. The heaviest rain on record, they said. An Act of God, the insurance companies called weather like that, and certainly it had been an almost biblical deluge. But surely God wouldn't have sent the rains just to reveal the body? The man whose corpse had been hidden in that ditch had got his deserts, that was for sure.

The body might have lain undiscovered for months, even

21

years, without yesterday's downpour. The man would have been reported as a missing person soon enough – MISPERs the police called them in the crime series on the box – but they wouldn't have found a body. And without a body, they wouldn't have known how the man had died. They might even have concluded that he'd gone away somewhere quiet and killed himself: God knows, he'd had enough reason to do something like that.

But as the murderer sat with head in hands and the minutes dragged past, it began to seem not a bad thing after all that the body had revealed itself at this point. Water cleansed things; it might have brought the corpse to light, but it would have removed evidence as well, no doubt. All kinds of tiny, unpreventable things on the skin and the clothing which might have tied the victim to its murderer. And the police wouldn't find much to help them on what was left of the body; there was nothing in the pockets, nothing at all. The band of tension which had tightened around the killer's forehead since the news of the discovery gradually eased a little. A few minutes later, the hands were cautiously removed from the temples they had clasped for so long.

There was an interview on the six o'clock news with the man who had taken charge of the case. This time, the murderer recorded the item, then played the tape back three times: there was nothing like being well prepared. This Superintendent Tucker gave the impression that he was used to television. He was urbane, well groomed, courteous to his interviewer's probings: the kind of man to get the police a good name and give the public confidence. His man-of-the-world smile said that he had been through all this before, that the police would work with due diligence, but you mustn't expect miracles. These were early days yet, he pointed out. Twice.

The murderer switched the set off and smiled slowly. They knew nothing.

Superintendent Tucker, front man and prize wanker (in Percy Peach's disloyal assessment) was making his television broadcast.

By six o'clock on that Tuesday evening, the identity of the victim had been established. It was dental records which gave them the information they would otherwise have arrived at by other and more circuitous routes. And without the need for a national trawl: the victim had been a client of a Brunton dentist. Forensic came up with the details very quickly, and within hours a local dental assistant, delighted to be drawn into the melodrama, found a match in her patients' records. Peach whistled his surprise at the news. "Are you sure? Yes, of course you are. We can't argue with the evidence of the mouth." He glanced down at the sheet in his hands, with its account of fillings and extractions. "Bit of a turn-up, though, isn't it? Has anyone told Wanker Willy upstairs?"

The young constable flinched at such nomenclature, glanced apprehensively towards the door of Peach's office. "No, sir. Superintendent Tucker said he was not to be disturbed after he'd gone into make-up for the television interview."

"Good. I'll tell him myself in due course." Percy glanced down at the sheet again. "Lovely set of choppers our friend had. Had he been reported missing?"

"No, sir. We checked the MISPERs again on the computer after this came in, but no one had been in to report anything."

"Hmm. Sad, that. Your mum would soon be in here bleating about you if you went missing, wouldn't she?"

The young man grinned. "My wife would, sir. Wouldn't leave it ten days, anyway."

Peach eyed the young face with disapproval. Married, and scarcely old enough to direct traffic or pinch shoplifters. "Aye, your wife would, for sure. Think you were off rogering a suspect, if you didn't report every twelve hours, I expect." Peach had no very high opinion of wives, his views being coloured by an experience which had been terminated eight years ago but was still vivid in his memory. "Has anyone checked why he wasn't reported missing?"

"Someone's been round to the home address, sir. Apparently he was on holiday."

"Holiday? You mean these buggers get holidays? I thought their life was one long holiday!" Percy's prejudices ran deep, in this case right back to his childhood. "I'll get round there myself, I think. Only way, if you want a job done properly." He sighed, theatrically but not unkindly. "Better get off home now, lad. Before that wife of yours reports you missing."

Superintendent Tucker congratulated himself that the interview had gone surprisingly well.

He had slipped out to the hairdresser that morning (nothing as crude as a barber for a man who dealt with the media), in anticipation of a request from the television people. Planning ahead, as he constantly told his staff, was vital in modern police work. His hair would have come out well under the lights, he thought, well groomed but with just that touch of grey at the temples which gave gravitas to his persona. He had rung home, so with luck his wife would have recorded the relevant two minutes – he made the excuse that he wanted to study his technique for future occasions.

Considering that he had had nothing to give them to add to the dramatic news of a body not as yet identified, the exchange with the young female presenter had gone well. He had managed to give her the impression of care and concern without in any way suggesting panic. Of course, unlike that oaf Peach, he respected women, knew how to handle these things. He couldn't quite see how they could rise to the higher ranks in the police force, but in other walks of life there was no reason why they should not play a full and useful part.

"Ah, thought I might just catch you, sir. Winding down after the rigours of performance, were you?" Tucker's musings as he put on his coat and prepared for his journey home were rudely shattered by the arrival of DI Peach, meeting him head-on in the doorway of his office.

"Won't it wait, Peach? I've had a trying day already."

"Yes, sir. Of course it will. Silly of me not to consider the stresses a man like you operates under. I'll see you in the morning."

Tucker peered at him suspiciously. It was unlike this bouncing ball of insubordination to be so co-operative. "All right. First thing in the morning, we'll—"

"It's just that we have an identification on the victim. I thought you might want to know as soon as possible. Before I briefed the rest of the team. But of course I should have realised . . ."

Tucker turned heavily, hopelessly, back into his office, slumping into his chair, wanting only to stem the flow of words from that relentlessly bright and energetic voice. "All right, Percy. You'd better tell me. Here and now."

"Yes, sir. Conscientious to a fault, as usual. Sorry to burden you with it, when I see you were away to a well-earned rest at home."

"Out with it, Percy. Don't bugger about!"

A rare departure from his mandarin's pose into the language of the station. A warning to Percy that even Tucker could be

25

pushed too far. But Peach would make him hop about a bit, even now. "Well, sir, it turns out it isn't a vagrant, after all."

"Not a vagrant?" Tucker looked blank for a moment, then remembered his ill-advised conjecture of the morning about the background of this victim. "I see. Well, who the hell is it, then?"

"It's a Roman Catholic priest, sir. Cause a bit of a furore that will, I shouldn't wonder, when we get the investigation under way."

Percy smiled at the wall above his chief's head in happy anticipation.

Four

"I'm Detective Inspector Peach and this is Detective Sergeant Blake." Percy was at his least intimidating, and Lucy smiled encouragement and sympathy at the elderly woman.

It mattered little. Martha Hargreaves had built her life round the service of men, and a special breed of men at that, and she scarcely noticed the young woman as she stood in the doorway of the presbytery of the Sacred Heart RC Church. She nodded an acknowledgement to Peach and led the way to the high Victorian room into which she had conducted so many visitors in the past. She had heard of feminism and knew something of its aims, but she invariably sniffed derisively at the mention of the word. She was a good sniffer, Martha, able to convey a wealth of derision by the briefest use of her well-trained nasal organ.

But on the morning after the revelation of the corpse's identity, she compelled nothing but sympathy. Her eyes were red with grief, hollowed into black circles; plainly she had slept little in the night which had passed since she heard the news. She had found a black dress, long out of fashion, in which to clothe her grief. A double row of jet beads sat at her throat; her hand strayed to them in the conversation which followed, almost as if her fingers were counting off the beads of a rosary. She would not sit until they had done so, standing over them for a moment as they subsided into the depths of the ancient tapestries of the long settee. She had a slight stoop, as if years of carrying trays for her master and his visitors had shaped her posture into permanent obeisance.

Peach said, "We understand you were the housekeeper of Father John Bickerstaffe."

She nodded, snatching at her sleeve, relieved when she eventually found the handkerchief she needed. It was a large, practical, man's handkerchief: this woman had lived for years in an environment where female vanities were discouraged. She blew her nose noisily, then said with a shuddering breath which only just kept a sob at bay, "I suppose there's no chance . . . ? I mean, you're sure it really is . . . ?"

"Yes, we're sure now, Miss Hargreaves. I'm afraid it really is Father Bickerstaffe. He was formally identified last night." Lucy wondered if she should offer to make a cup of tea, then understood immediately the outrage which would be caused by any attempt to breach the walls of this woman's kitchen.

Martha Hargreaves nodded, dabbing briefly at the red eyes with the big handkerchief. "His brother identified him, I suppose." She felt relieved that she had been spared that ordeal at least, and yet obscurely deprived. It seemed wrong that the man her priest had seen so seldom should be accorded this final, intimate duty ahead of her.

Lucy Blake said, "Yes, it was Father Bickerstaffe's brother who did the identification; it's usually a close relative who has to do it. It was no more than a formality, really, but the law demands these things. Miss Hargreaves, I'm afraid I have to tell you that we think Father Bickerstaffe's death was a suspicious one. You understand what that means?"

"Yes. You mean somebody killed him." Surprisingly, the idea that he had died in this way did not seem to shock or appal her as they had expected: her grief was all for the man's death, not for the manner of it. Perhaps she was going to be more help to them than they had anticipated when they arranged this routine meeting. The tears Martha Hargreaves thought she had exhausted during the night ran anew now as she confronted the nature of this death, and she dabbed hastily at her face with the handkerchief.

Lucy Blake glanced at Peach, then went into the form of words which had become familiar in cases like this. It made her realise what a lonely life the celibate priest's can be, for this was a routine usually reserved for grieving relatives, not housekeepers. "When we think that someone has been unlawfully killed, we have to try to build up a picture of the life he led, of the people who surrounded him. It's the only sort of crime where the victim isn't available for questioning, you see. It makes people like you very important to us, Miss Hargreaves."

The housekeeper nodded, drawing herself a little more erect within the wooden arms of the upright armchair she had chosen for herself. "He was a good man, Father was. A kind man. Always available to people when there was trouble. Always very good when there was a death in the family." Her breath caught at that, as she thought again of her employer's own death. "Everybody says that about him. A great comfort when there was a death, Father Bickerstaffe was. Thoughtful about people. Understanding. Don't let anyone tell you otherwise. Don't let them take that away from him."

There was something here, some unexpected reservation about the man of whom she spoke so fondly. Others, she was hinting, would not be so kind in their memories of Father Bickerstaffe. But she was too upset for them to go straight to it. It would come out, in due course, if they let her talk,

Lucy Blake decided. You had to be like a doctor, sometimes, listening and waiting, paying regard to what was unsaid as well as the straightforward revelations. It was one of the few aspects of interviewing in which she felt superior to Percy Peach. Lucy said, "Tell us about the life Father Bickerstaffe lived here, Martha, about the work he did and the work you did to keep the place running smoothly."

The last phrase brought a small, unexpected smile to the housekeeper's lips. "That's what I tried to do, you know. Keep the place running smoothly while Father went about his work. They're only men, after all, aren't they, even if they're rather special men?"

For a moment the old housekeeper was a conspirator in her gender with the pretty, green-blue eyed young woman who had come into her kingdom to question her. Lucy sensed in that instant that this woman had endured a hard life, of unremitting toil and service, with no regular hours and no union to plead her case.

But it was Inspector Peach who took things forward. Percy had been brought up a Catholic, but had discarded the religion when he was eighteen and exploring the delights of girls. He now said with uncharacteristic gentleness, "Tell us a little about Father Bickerstaffe's life. He said Mass every morning, I expect."

"Yes. Seven thirty every morning, nine and ten thirty on Sundays. There's an evening mass on Sundays as well, but usually Father Arkwright comes down from St Mary's to say that. I go to the morning mass, most weekdays. There aren't more than ten or twelve of us, most times."

"You live on the premises?"

"Yes. I have my own little flat upstairs. My own bathroom and sitting room." She sounded defiant as she said it. She might be out of touch with the world and its wicked ways, but she wasn't blind enough to have missed all the speculation about priests and their housekeepers. Well, you couldn't accuse her of anything in that line, not at any time during the thirty years she'd worked in this presbytery with three different parish priests. Nor poor Father Bickerstaffe, for that matter. No one had muttered about anything of that kind. Perhaps if he'd had someone like this open-faced, attractive girl to share his bed, all might have been well . . . Martha surprised herself with that daring liberal thought; she certainly couldn't claim to be an expert in such matters.

Lucy said, "Can you give us some idea of the rest of his day after Mass, please?"

"Well, he'd have breakfast at about nine, or just before. He'd been settling for this muesli stuff and toast, lately; I always made him a cooked breakfast when he first came here."

"And when would that be, Miss Hargreaves?"

"Eight years ago." The answer came very promptly. "He'd been a curate over in Preston, but I think they thought he deserved his own parish, even though he was still young. He was only thirty-two when he came here, you know." She said it as proudly as if he had been her son. Then her face clouded a little, as if she wondered whether she should have revealed anything as intimate as a priest's age to these strangers.

"And he was the only priest working here on a regular basis?"

"Yes. We could get help from St Mary's when we wanted it – they have four priests there. But it wasn't often that Father asked them to help out. We're still quite a small parish, in spite of the new building. But it's a busy one, with the school and the youth club."

"Yes, it must be. Busy life for you too, I expect."

"Well, I made tea for all Father's visitors, if he asked me to. And some of my sponge cake or scones, for most of them. I bake two or three times a week."

"When did these visitors come here?"

"In the mornings, those of them that could. And the rest in the evenings – mainly those who were working and couldn't come during the day. Father liked to clear the decks so that he had most of the day to himself for other things."

"What other things, Martha?" Peach came in a fraction too quickly as he sensed the possibility of contacts which might be important.

Martha Hargreaves looked at him with suspicion, then gave one of her disapproving sniffs. "Visiting the sick. Comforting the bereaved. Mostly things like that. He went into our little school too, about once a week, to see if he could help the headmistress with any of the problems there."

Peach, who thirty years ago had had his seven-year-old calves smacked regularly with a ruler in a Catholic junior school by a woman who looked not unlike Miss Hargreaves, considered this impeccable catalogue of moral services dolefully. Not much chance of a murderer among such contacts, though he made a mental note to interview the headmistress personally. "What about the youth club? Presumably most of the activities there were conducted in the evenings?"

"Yes. You'd have to ask others about that. I never set foot in the place."

Something very strange had happened to the housekeeper of the late Father John Bickerstaffe, Peach noticed. A curtain had dropped over the grief-stricken face, a curtain which carried upon it the message that no information would be given about this area, however fervently it might be sought. Something here then, thought Percy, in his suspicious policeman's way.

An area worth digging over, with or without the help of this guardian of the late priest's reputation. "Went across to the club on most evenings, did he?"

"Father Bickerstaffe put in an appearance there on most evenings, yes. It was his idea to open the place, and I'm sure it was most successful."

"Really. And how many nights a week was it open?" Peach, encountering resistance and feeling as a result that a rather more aggressive style was justified, was much more at home.

"Four nights. Wednesdays to Saturdays. Father heard confession until seven thirty on Wednesdays and Saturdays, and some of the other evenings he had visitors, as I said, but he liked to get into the club for the last hour whenever he could."

"Which was?"

"Nine to ten." Martha found she was being made to talk more about the place than she had ever intended, but you couldn't refuse them straight facts like this. And they were trying to find out who had killed poor gentle Father Bickerstaffe, weren't they? You had to help them where you could.

"Bit early for a youth club to shut, isn't it?"

"I don't know about that." Her lips set for a moment into the thin line they'd formed when the club was first mentioned. "They're only young, you know, the kids who use it. Most of these teenagers seem to want to drink and go to these disco places when they're not much more than children, nowadays."

If not worse, the two CID people thought. "About eleven to fourteen, would you say, the ages in the youth club?"

"I couldn't say, I'm sure." Then, when they didn't comment and she felt her own recalcitrance weighing upon her, she said,

"They were allowed to join at eleven, when they left our junior school and went on to the secondary. Father said it would mark their growing up but help to keep them together as a group." She brought out the words carefully, pleased with herself for remembering the phrase she had heard her employer use so many months before. "I don't know what age they are when they leave, but I know Father was upset because so many of them stopped coming when they were still quite young."

"What kind of activities went on over there?"

"I don't know, I'm sure. Table tennis and darts, I believe. And I think they use the school hall for badminton sometimes. But you'll have to ask someone else, if you think it's important. I never go into the place." They'd made her talk more about it than she'd intended, after all. But she couldn't think she'd said anything really important.

Peach nodded almost imperceptibly at his Detective Sergeant, and Lucy Blake resumed the questioning. "You liked Father Bickerstaffe, Martha. We can tell that."

"He was a lovely man. Very considerate. He even tried to wash up for me, when we were busy, but I didn't let him, of course." A tear sprang from her left eye and ran slow and unchecked down her cheek at the memory, whilst the sodden handkerchief turned in her hands.

"Then you'll be anxious that we find whoever was responsible for his death." Even now, Lucy shied away from the brutality of the word 'murder', though they knew that it was surely that. "If you want us to find out who killed him, it means answering our questions, as fully and as frankly as you can."

"Yes. I know that."

"Do you know anyone who might have wanted to kill Father Bickerstaffe, Martha?"

"No. No, I don't." It was inconceivable to Martha Hargreaves that anyone could ever contemplate the enormous sin of killing a priest, and least of all kind and gentle Father Bickerstaffe.

"But someone did, Martha. In all probability, someone he knew. Perhaps someone who had come here in the weeks before he was killed."

A little shudder ran right through the shapeless frame beneath the black weeds. "I don't see how I can help you."

"Did Father Bickerstaffe have a diary or a list of his engagements? We need to know both the people who came here and those he went out to meet, you see."

"Yes. He had a red book with 'Engagement Diary' on the front of it. He kept it on his desk, but I never looked inside it."

"No, of course you didn't. But we need to take it away with us now, you see."

"You can't. Father took it with him when – when he went away." She was beset by a series of sobs and dabbed almost angrily with the handkerchief at her blotched face. "Sorry."

Peach waited until she regained a measure of composure before he said softly, "How long is it since he was here, Martha?"

"Two weeks. Two weeks ago today, he went away. Father Lloyd has been coming in from St Mary's to say Mass, but he doesn't have any meals here, or stay around to see anyone."

"Why did Father Bickerstaffe go away, Martha? Was it a holiday?"

"I don't know. Yes, I think it was a holiday. He hadn't had a holiday for a long time." But she sounded as if she was trying to convince herself that it was so by her repetition of the word.

"And where did he go to?"

"I don't know. The clergy arrange these things among themselves. Perhaps he was staying in another presbytery, with one of his friends."

"I see. He had a lot of friends among his fellow priests, did he?"

"Quite a few. They played golf sometimes, over at Pleasington or Preston. He didn't play all that often, but he enjoyed it. I think he was quite good." A stubborn pride stole over her face as she said it, as if she spoke again of the child she had never had.

"We shall need a list of all these people, Martha. It's a pity his desk diary isn't here: we'll have to ask you to remember all the names you can, and tell us everything you know about them. I know it's going to be—"

Peach broke off as the phone shrilled loudly in the lofty hall beyond the heavy door. Martha Hargreaves said immediately, "I must answer that," and started up from her chair in undisguised relief.

She shut the door carefully behind her. They could just hear her muffled tones beyond the thick mahogany panels. She came back full of awe at the status of her caller. "It's the bishop," she said in a tone which others might have reserved for royalty. "I told him I was talking with the police about what had happened to Father. He says he wants to speak to you himself."

Peach went to the phone and gave his name and rank briskly, refusing to submit to the aura a bishop had carried in his childhood – hadn't he been the only man who could sanction mixed marriages? Bishop Hogan had no trace of the Irish brogue Percy subconsciously expected in Roman Catholic clergy. His quiet, educated, English voice said, "I believe you're investigating the death of Father John Bickerstaffe.

As his spiritual director, I should like to speak to you as soon as possible. I think you will find what I have to say useful. And I would rather you heard it from me than from anyone else."

Five

"Ah, good morning, sir. We've seen the housekeeper. We're off to see the Bishop now. Sounds like a joke, doesn't it?" DI Peach beamed his cheerful energy full into the face of Superintendent Tucker, Head of Brunton CID.

Tucker shuddered inwardly at the thought of this modern Attila trampling over the hierarchy of the oldest church in Christendom. "Come into my office for a moment, will you, Percy?"

Peach followed him dutifully. Tucker didn't often use his Christian name, and the false bonhomie invariably indicated nervousness, a failing Peach was happy to detect in friend or foe. This time Tucker actually asked him to sit down, as if he felt obscurely that this might slow the headlong pace of the Inspector's advance upon the world outside. "Just a friendly word of warning, Percy," he said uneasily.

"Yes, sir. Much appreciated, I'm sure. Your overview always is. I always say to the lads when the going gets tough, 'You might think that while you're out here with the water coming over your wellies and the shit seeping into your socks that Mr Tucker is sitting in the station doing fuck all, but what we're getting is his overview of things, and that's very important to us. You may not see it right now,' I say, 'but—'"

"Peach!"

"Yes, sir?"

"Shut up and listen, will you."

"Yes, sir. Sorry, sir." Peach's round face shone with a mixture of remorse and rapt attention. Tommy Bloody Tucker might know he was insolent, but he also knew he couldn't do without him, if he wanted to preserve the clear-up rate on which his reputation depended.

Tucker found it difficult to concentrate with that round moon of devotion on the other side of his desk. "I don't want to impede the pace of your investigation; I've always given you a free rein, and I shall continue to do so. That's the way I operate my teams. But if there is a problem, it's my job to spot it and advise you of it."

He's losing his thread, thought Percy delightedly. He doesn't like my interruptions, but he can't go on without them. Thank you, God, if you are up there after all. DI Peach allowed a degree of puzzlement to creep into the intensity of his expression, then leaned forward two inches more, as if endeavouring to correct his own crassness by the extra effort to understand.

Tucker shut his eyes desperately. "And in this case the thing is, Percy, er . . ."

"Yes, sir? The thing is, sir?"

"Bishop!" said Tucker, desperately and vehemently, as if the word had relieved a blockage in his throat in the nick of time.

"Ah, yes, sir." Percy seized upon the word triumphantly. "The Bishop. You want me to rough him up a bit? Show him he can't trifle with Brunton CID just because he has a purple uniform? You can rely on me, sir. If he doesn't give us every co-operation, I'll stick him in a cell for an hour or two, let him kick his heels until he comes to his senses. He might think he's some kind of VIP, but with your authority behind me I'll soon show him which way the—"

"No, Peach, no!" The appalled Tucker held up both hands to stem the flow of this mistaken torrent. "You misunderstand me. What I wanted to say is that we must go easy on the Bishop. Handle him with kid gloves."

Percy's face looked baffled, as if he had never heard these tired clichés before. "Go easy on him, sir," he repeated slowly. "Handle him with kid gloves." His brow furrowed with the effort. Then his expression lightened. "You mean lure him into indiscretions? That's a good idea, sir. I'm sure they're easy meat for that, these celibate clergy. I'll get DS Blake to wear a mini-skirt and black nylons. Flash him a bit of the old gusset when she crosses her legs, like Sharon Stone. She's a bit sensitive about these gender things, but I'm sure she'll do it, if I tell her the order's come from you. Bet he falls for it, too. There's lots of jokes about actresses and bishops – I can never remember them, but I expect you pass lots of them around within the Lodge. Well, I must say, it's another of your original ideas, and I expect it will work. Well worth a try, anyway, and—"

"*Peach! I didn't mean that!*" In the big CID room below them, where lesser mortals operated without their own offices, male and female officers looked at each other, and understood that Peach was winding up the governor again. Tucker felt the pulse in his temple and made himself speak quietly. "That's the very point I'm trying to make. You go charging in, treading on all kinds of sensitive toes, and it's me who has to pick up the pieces!" Percy tried looking puzzled anew at this crashing mix of metaphors, but Tucker was well beyond such linguistic niceties. "The Catholic Church is an important institution, Peach, and we must treat it accordingly."

"You don't mean they're to have special privileges, sir?" Peach tried out the very whited sepulchre expression he had deplored in Tucker on public occasions, and beamed it full upon his chief. "In my book, murder is murder, and I couldn't be a party to any cover-ups for the sake of race, rank or religion." He enunciated the three R-words with the fervour of a politician.

"I don't want cover-ups," said Tucker desperately. "All I want is a little diplomacy."

"Diplomacy, sir?"

"Yes, Peach, diplomacy. The Catholic church is very big in this area. One in seven people round here are Catholics, the highest proportion in Great Britain. We don't want to be accused of prejudice, do we? Now, the fact that you may not understand this religion and its adherents should make you tread very carefully. You've no idea what you're dealing with, and therefore it behoves you to—"

"Ah, but I have, sir. I was born a papist, you see. I was a left-footer with the best of them until about the time I joined the force. I know all about the corruptions and the scandals of what we used to call Holy Mother Church. I could tell you things about the Irish Christian Brothers that would—"

"*Don't!* For God's sake, Peach, go carefully."

"For God's sake? Yes, I see, sir."

"But you don't, Peach, do you? You don't seem to understand that we have to tread cautiously in the community nowadays. Whether you like it or not, we have an image to preserve."

"An image, yes, sir." Peach allowed the troubled look to creep back into his earnest features. "But wouldn't that be best served by finding the murderer and arresting him? I can't quite see how hushing things up is going to help our image,

41

especially when the Press find out that we've been told to go easy on the clergy in case we upset the left-footers. Of course, you're in charge, as always, but—"

"I didn't say hush things up, did I?" Tucker found himself shouting again in his frustration. People were always telling him how acute this man Peach was, and yet here he was threatening to destroy the police image his Superintendent had so carefully fostered in the higher echelons of the local community. Tucker controlled his voice with difficulty, made himself speak slowly. "I said proceed with care, that's all. We don't want the Catholic community saying we have a particular prejudice against them. I'm asking you to bear that in mind when you talk to people like bishops, that's all."

"No third degree then, sir?"

"No. Certainly not."

"And no waving knickers at him?"

"No." Tucker closed his eyes and tried to control the shudder this picture gave him.

"Not even a quick flash of gusset to—"

"Nothing of that sort at all, please."

Peach wondered for a moment whether to go on to nuns, then decided that he had already wasted enough time on this humourless windbag. "You wouldn't like to interview the bishop yourself, sir?"

For a moment, Tucker was tempted, in the light of the awful things Peach had been threatening. But it was too long since he had been at the crime face for him to start working at it again now. He bridled as always at the suggestion of real work on the case of which he was nominally in charge, as Percy had known he would. "No. You know my policy is not to interfere, and I shall stick to it. I'm just giving you guidance as to how you are to proceed."

"Yes, sir. Valuable guidance, as I'm sure we'll see, when this is all over and our killer is behind bars. I'll convey your overview to the team, when we meet next."

And Percy Peach, who lived in the real world and had always planned to treat the bishop with proper deference, went happily downstairs.

The murderer of Father John Bickerstaffe watched the one o'clock television news and was shaken.

Events were moving quickly. When you weren't used to these things, when you knew nothing about police procedures, you weren't prepared for such efficiency, such rapid deployment of resources. The body had already been identified. There was a still photograph of the church where the priest had worked, then a sequence of the children going into the little Catholic junior school next door to it. That wasn't fair: it connected this man with innocence, gave the impression that he had been quietly going about his work as a pastor when he was brutally interrupted in the pursuit of his duties.

Of course, it made a good story for the Press, and that was all they were interested in. They didn't know what had caused Bickerstaffe's death yet. When they did, they'd sing a different tune.

But it was worrying, all the same, when you had expected that months or years might have passed before all this attention began. You thought you'd been careful enough, but you could never be quite sure. Thirty officers on the case, they said; it seemed a huge number, when you were only one. You thought you'd covered your traces, been cool and diligent, but it was disturbing, none the less, to find the hunt under way so soon, and being pursued so vigorously.

The murderer went over what had been done for the hundredth time, without finding a flaw which could lead to discovery. Nothing there to incriminate you, if you kept your nerve. That was going to be tested soon now – much sooner than anticipated. But there would be other suspects, plenty of others, and there was no reason why this crime should not go down as unsolved, if you kept your nerve.

The police would be coming now, within days – perhaps even within hours. The interview would be an ordeal, but there was no way they could be certain it was you, if you didn't make a mistake. By the end of the afternoon, the murderer was almost impatient to have it over with.

The killer would have been interested, very interested, in the information which was being delivered to the police while the television showed its pictures of church and school. Despite new headquarters which were only three years old, the Brunton police were already short of space. The murder room had been set up in a Portacabin at one end of the station car park. It was here that a Detective Sergeant was collating information on his computer when he took the call from the forensic laboratory at Chorley.

"Interesting chaps, maggots," said the cheerful voice after it had introduced itself. "Develop at a uniform rate. Very useful for men like us who poke about inside dead bodies. And the weather in the two weeks before Monday's downpour was nicely consistent for us. Warm and dry; low seventies by day, mid-fifties by night. Means we can be reasonably certain about the rate of maturing of this particular collection of busy little chaps. I'd say your man was killed a minimum of ten days before you found him. In fact, I'd be prepared to say between ten and twelve days under oath in court – not as a fact of course, but as informed scientific opinion. I don't think I'd have many arguments about it from my colleagues."

DS Jackson made a careful note of it. Probable date of death, Thursday 20th or Friday 21st August, according to specialist forensic entomologist at Chorley. A day either way, at most. Two or three days after the priest had left his church, then. Knowing how Peach would react if he didn't get everything he could out of the scientists, the DS said hastily, "Anything else you can give us yet?"

The forensic entomologist refused to go beyond his specialist area, but passed him on to another, more proletarian, but equally cheerful voice. "Very little, I'm afraid. People think water is hygienic, and I suppose it is, in the ordinary way of things, but it's a bloody nuisance for us forensic chaps. We haven't finished the examination of the clothes and hair yet, but I doubt if we're are going to find any useful fibres. There's a smear of grease on the back of the sweater – how recent and what the source is we don't know, but we're working on it. You'll have the full report in a couple of days."

DS Jackson thanked them for the prompt service. He knew there was a six to eight week backlog of work at the Home Office laboratory. But other things were put aside for murder.

Percy Peach drove over the moors towards Manchester with lively expectations. In his multifarious criminal investigations, it had never fallen to him before to visit a Bishop.

But the Bishop's residence was a disappointment to him. In the Church of England he knew they called them Bishops' Palaces, and this had led him to expect an altogether grander and more interesting building than this. More like a doctor's surgery in one of those group practices, he thought, as he parked his car carefully in the only available space outside it.

Bishop Hogan's residence was a modern red-brick building, rectangular and without external decorations. True, it was large enough to whet the appetite of critics who detected opulence among the princes of the church whilst their flocks starved in the third world, but even that proved an illusion on entry through the blue double doors. This was plainly a working building, the bureaucratic centre of a busy diocese – Tucker had been right when he said that they were in the most Catholic part of England. Word-processors hummed in the room with an open door on his right, and he even caught a glimpse of women at work in what he had anticipated would be an all-male environment.

On his left, a sign on the door said, 'Bishop's Chaplain'. It was from this room that a young man in a bright green pullover emerged and said, "You must be Detective Inspector Peach. His Grace is expecting you." He smiled at Lucy Blake, standing behind the Inspector; Peach thought it was a standard assessment of the talent, until he realised that the young man wore a clerical collar beneath his brightly efficient smile.

The bishop was a man in his fifties, with a domed forehead which gave a hint of asceticism to his tall presence. He wore purple silk, which was revealed in its full glory as he rose and came round his desk to meet them. The uniform even extended to the small purple skull-cap on his distinguished head; Tucker would have approved of his image, thought Peach. He resisted an absurd compulsion to fall on one knee and kiss the Bishop's ring – the last time he had met a Bishop, he had been an unworthy candidate for confirmation amidst the breathy guilts of puberty.

He introduced DS Blake. Lucy was ready to shake hands, but the Bishop merely nodded his acknowledgement of her name. She noticed his beautifully manicured nails, longer than her own, and wondered how long it was since Bishop Hogan had last washed the dishes. Percy fought down an impulse towards deference which was wholly foreign to his normal behaviour, and said, "You have things to tell us about the late Father Bickerstaffe, I believe."

"I have indeed. Excuse the full regalia: I have an engagement as soon as we have finished here. Do sit down." Bishop Hogan indicated a choice of comfortable chairs with a wide sweep of his episcopal arm. It was a large room, with a high, stuccoed ceiling from an earlier era and windows on three sides. From the number of seats available, it seemed that it was used for informal meetings of various kinds. Peach and Blake perched gingerly on the edge of wide, deeply upholstered armchairs. Dangerous chairs, in Percy's opinion: you could settle back in one of these and fall asleep during one of Tommy Bloody Tucker's interminable briefings.

There was no danger of that with Bishop Hogan. He was ready to come straight to the point; if they had only known it, he was as anxious to have this conversation over and done with as his visitors were. But first there was a rattle of teacups in the corridor outside. The Bishop's chaplain took over the wagon from the aproned woman at the door and pushed it rather self-consciously into the room. Good sign that, thought the experienced DI Peach: confidential information, not suitable for tea-ladies' ears, must surely be on offer very shortly.

He was right. The Bishop waited until they each had a home-made cake and a cup of tea to balance, then nodded to his chaplain to withdraw. He said, "First let me check my facts. I understand that you are treating Father Bickerstaffe's death as suspicious."

Peach nodded. "And that, as you probably know, is police-speak for saying we think he was murdered. I can tell you that we are now quite certain that Father Bickerstaffe was killed by person or persons unknown, some ten to twelve days before his body was found. As yet, we have no idea who that person or persons might be. We are trying to build up some kind of picture of the sort of man Father Bickerstaffe was and how he lived out the last months of his life."

The Bishop nodded sadly. "Which is why I contacted you and asked you to be so kind as to come here."

A diplomat, this man, thought Percy; with his ascetic good looks and his polished grasp of procedure, he might have been an ambassador in lay life, or even a politician, if he had chosen to misuse his social skills. Not many people greeted a police visit with the thought that they had been kind enough to come here. He said with a trace of his normal aggression, "Anything you have to say about the dead man at this stage will be useful to us. You shouldn't hold anything back."

The bishop smiled. This squat and aggressive little man seemed a little nervous in his presence; brought up a Catholic, he shouldn't wonder. Bishop Hogan was an expert by now at recognising the symptoms, which usually involved an uneasy combination of a residual deference from childhood and a determination to be brusque and treat a church dignitary with as much consideration as the local grocer. "I have no intention of holding anything back, Inspector. I shall say what I have to say, then answer any questions you may have as fully as I can. Now, I understand that you have already visited Miss Hargreaves at the Presbytery at St Thomas's. Indeed, I know you have, for you were there when I spoke to you this morning. What did you learn from Miss Hargreaves?"

Percy glanced instinctively at DS Blake. These days, he

tended not to assume that they were in agreement unless they had already discussed the matter. She gave him no more than the slightest of answering smiles and he said, "Precious little, really. We learned that his housekeeper genuinely liked him, that she thought he was a good parish priest. That he worked hard, was good with the sick and the bereaved. Not much else. Nothing that seems likely to be of much use to us, if you want me to be honest, Your Grace. It's a sad thing perhaps, but in these circumstances, we have to be more interested in the enemies people had than their friends, more interested in their vices than their virtues. If they have given people reasons to hate them, whether real or imaginary, we need to know about that side of their lives. Every mother thinks her son is a saint, and Martha Hargreaves was a little too much like a mother in that respect to be much use to us. It may be your job to see the good in people, especially when you're speaking to the relatives of the dead; I'm afraid in this job we spend a lot of our time looking for dead people's vices."

Bishop Hogan smiled. "Of course you do. And we're not as blinkered to wickedness as you might think. I've spent a lot of my life trying to resolve how God can be infinitely just and infinitely merciful at the same time. Fortunately, you don't have to wrestle with such things. But perhaps we're not so far apart. We both have to give attention to the way people behave and the reasons why they do things." He set his empty cup down firmly on the low table between them and watched approvingly as Lucy Blake did the same. She pulled out her notebook and the small gold pen which was her gesture to femininity. "There are things about Father Bickerstaffe which you need to know, which I hope you will treat with as much discretion as possible."

Percy bridled a little at that. "We shall treat whatever you

49

tell us as confidential, as long as that remains within our control. If it affects the outcome of our investigation, it may not be possible to keep information confidential. If we are successful, there will no doubt be a court case in due course, and things may have to emerge in evidence. You will realise that we cannot control what use lawyers may make of material which we may see as only background to our enquiries."

It was a little too stiff, a little too long. Lucy was amused to see that Percy, who so delighted in discomforting interviewees himself, should suddenly become awkward and circumspect in front of this urbane figure in purple. Perhaps the Bishop felt it too. He nodded a little absently, steepled his long fingers, said quietly, "As John Bickerstaffe's spiritual director, I have been drawn into the events which dominated the last months of his life. It is a wretched business, though unfortunately by no means a unique one. In this case, it has ended in tragedy, and the nature of this death means that I must tell you everything I know which might be of relevance to your enquiries." He sighed. "Did Miss Hargreaves mention the youth club at St Hugh's?"

Peach nodded, anticipating by now some of what was to come. 'Never presume too much. Never jump ahead of the evidence, or you'll jump to the wrong conclusions,' his first guv'nor, a man as different from Tucker as anthracite is from balsa wood, had told him. For a naturally impatient man, it was good advice, and Percy reminded himself of it still whenever he was tempted towards short cuts. But there was nothing wrong with pushing people forward a bit. "Martha Hargreaves mentioned the club all right. She spoke of the little Sacred Heart primary school beside the church as well; she seemed happier with that. She didn't seem to want to say much about the youth club."

Bishop Hogan smiled. "Miss Hargreaves is a loyal supporter of Father Bickerstaffe. And I've no doubt that he was very kind to her. But like all of us, he had his weaknesses, Inspector."

"And Bickerstaffe's was boys?"

The grey episcopal eyebrows rose a fraction over the deep-set eyes. "Yes. May I ask how you knew that it wasn't girls?"

Peach shrugged, trying not to look pleased with himself. "I didn't. It's just with celibate priests, boys are statistically much more probable. Of course, when it's adult sex that interests them, they're far more likely to run off with a buxom lady parishioner, but—"

"Quite!" The Bishop hastily interrupted what he feared might become a catalogue of the weaknesses with which he was all too familiar after ten years in the busiest Catholic diocese in England. "Well, I have to tell you that your surmise is correct. Unfortunately, Father Bickerstaffe was tempted towards the boys in his youth club. Even more unfortunately, he failed to resist this temptation." He looked unhappily towards Lucy Blake as she quietly turned to a new sheet in her notebook, then nodded sadly.

Peach said softly, "We need the names of all of the children concerned. I think you know that. And also some account of times, and how these things were brought to light. This is the kind of grievance I spoke of just now. A parent defending a child is capable of all sorts of violence."

The Bishop said slowly, "Or in this case revenging a child. I'm afraid that there's no doubt of John Bickerstaffe's guilt in the area. He confessed it to me in this very room, not much more than a month ago." He was silent for a moment as he remembered the weeping, hysterical figure whom he had needed to revive with sharp words and brandy. The only image of the dead man he could now remember was the small bald patch he had never before noticed on the bowed forty-year-old head, which had sobbed so violently above the thin shoulders. And now John Bickerstaffe was gone, and this tough little Inspector was sitting in the same chair he had occupied. It seemed ironic that the officer who might so easily have been hounding the unhappy priest into court was now searching for the man who had killed him. Or the woman: bishops, like policemen, saw enough of human vice to make that reservation automatically.

Peach repeated, "We shall need names. And all the information you can give us about times and places."

Bishop Hogan gave them four names. He could not be certain that the list was comprehensive, but he thought so. It was the usual story in such cases. He had known nothing until the first whisper came to him, three months earlier, from the parish priest of St Mary's, in Brunton. A single mother with four children had complained that the eldest of them had been indecently assaulted by Father Bickerstaffe, when he had stayed behind to tidy up the youth club with the priest one Thursday night. Once she had spoken to Canon O'Leary, once the taboo on this awful, unthinkable priestly vice had been broken, she had obviously whispered to others. And found that once the news was abroad, other cases emerged.

Children do not know how to cope with the horror of abuse; they blame themselves and keep quiet. Percy Peach and Lucy Blake knew that; Bishop Hogan knew that. But the children, of course, did not know. Once the first victim had broken his silence, four others were unearthed quite quickly by the urgent questionings of newly alarmed parents.

Lucy Blake noted the names from the Bishop's file, then said quietly, "How far did the abuse go? Was there full penetration?"

Bishop Hogan, who had thought himself unshockable by now, was thrown out of his stride by this. He had expected the question, had been thankful indeed that it had been couched in such clinical terms, but he had not expected it to come from a woman, and a young and attractive woman at that. Among even the most sophisticated of Catholic clergy, the images of the Madonna have been installed deep in the psyche during childhood.

He thrust away another of his preconceptions. "No. Not in any of the cases, as far as we have been able to ascertain. That is what the children said, and what John Bickerstaffe eventually confirmed." He looked at the expectant faces, knew that he must go on. "He touched the boys' private parts, made them touch his. As far as I can gather, he encouraged the boys to help him masturbate, but didn't insist upon it when they seemed really distressed. I don't know how much detail you—"

"No more than that, at the moment," said Peach briskly. "But this is the first we've heard of any of this. Weren't these offences coming to court?"

The Bishop, though he had expected this, looked embarrassed. "They might have done. That would have depended on the people involved. We had removed the source of evil. We were still discussing the issue with the parents. If they could be assured that the offender would not commit this particular sin again, it might be better that the issue did not end in a court of law. It is an appalling experience for children to have to give evidence, I'm sure you'll agree."

"And appalling publicity for the Church of Rome," said Peach dryly. The words were out before he knew they were coming.

Bishop Hogan nodded sadly. "I don't deny that. But perhaps you would agree that the churches, with all their faults, are still influences for the good in a flawed society. Unless the publicity such cases inevitably carry is necessary to the cause of justice, it may not serve a useful purpose."

Something in that, Percy reluctantly agreed. But I bet you've offered these wretched parents money to buy them off from legal action, he thought, and money always muddies moral issues. He said, "Well, that's not our concern, I'm glad to say. Our only business today is to gather information which may help us to find out who killed Father Bickerstaffe, and you've certainly given us some of that. One more thing. We know that Father Bickerstaffe had left St Hugh's some days before he died. But we don't know where he was actually living at the time of his death."

"No. He had been sent to Downton Hall. It's a house we keep for retired clergy in the Ribble Valley. It's also used by priests who are recovering from serious illnesses."

And by those who have caused such embarrassment to the Church that they have to be removed from office and hidden away, thought Percy. He said dryly, "Presumably this place is fairly remote."

"Yes. Father Walsh, my secretary, will show you its position on the map." The Bishop had anticipated this, obviously. "It isn't very far from the place where the body of John Bickerstaffe was found."

"How many people knew he was there?"

"I and my secretary, plus Monsignor Eaton, who runs Downton Hall. But I can't guarantee that other people couldn't have found out. Probably most clergy in the diocese would surmise that a priest in trouble in his parish would be sent to Downton. They are usually discreet in these matters, but they're not sworn to secrecy. It might surprise you to know that priests gossip among themselves as much as the rest of society,

Inspector. Pieces of scandal pass round fairly quickly. It's part of being lonely." The Bishop allowed himself a sad smile.

Peach looked at the long, reflective face above the purple silk for a moment. "Bishop Hogan, we now know that Father Bickerstaffe had been dead for about ten days before his body was actually discovered. Yet no one had reported his disappearance. Why was that?"

Bishop Hogan sighed. "I think I must bear the responsibility for that. I was informed that John Bickerstaffe had disappeared twenty-four hours after it happened. We didn't inform you because we thought he'd gone away to think things out for himself. All cases differ, but that's not unusual for a priest in trouble. John had been warned that he might have to give up his priesthood, to seek a different kind of life somewhere else. It turns a priest's life on its head. Like many Catholic clergy, John had relatives in Ireland. It was suggested to me that he might have gone there to contemplate his next step, but we weren't able to check on that: we had no addresses."

Lucy Blake looked up from her notebook. "Did you think he might have gone quietly away to commit suicide?"

It was a thought which might have been better left unvoiced, but Bishop Hogan did not flinch from it, nor bridle at the presumption of this fresh-faced young woman. "And relieved us all of an embarrassment, you mean? Of course we were aware of the possibility that a man in John's position might take his own life. Suicide is always a temptation for those under great mental stress. But despair is still the ultimate sin for us Catholics, and the pressures against suicide are strongest of all for a Catholic priest. Suicides happen occasionally, but they are very rare."

His frankness gave a dignity to his pronouncement. Peach,

who had wanted to ask just when the missing priest's disappearance would eventually have been reported, decided that the question would serve no useful purpose. He stood up abruptly. "Thank you for your help. And thank you for the refreshments. We may need to come back to you for more information after we've spoken to some of the parents you've named for us."

By this time, all three of them were glad to end this meeting. The two CID representatives had driven ten miles and the car was climbing up towards the moors on the other side of Bolton before Lucy Blake said quietly, "I don't like child abusers. They take advantage of those who can't fight back."

Peach's hand stole towards hers, covered it for a moment, gave it a small squeeze, which might have been consolation, might have been appreciation. They drove another mile before he said, "Neither do I. But you've got to like murderers even less. It's part of the job."

Six

In twelve years of supervising Scene of Crime teams, Detective Sergeant Joe Jackson had never before visited a presbytery. And in forty years of housekeeping for a succession of priests, Martha Hargreaves had never taken anyone, let alone a policeman, into the private quarters of a minister of the Lord. The two regarded each other with mutual suspicion.

Jackson took a deep breath and plunged into the phrases he had used a hundred times before. "I'm afraid we have to search the premises. It's in case we can find anything which might be useful. It's what a Scene of Crime team does, Mrs Hargreaves."

"It's Miss Hargreaves. And there was no crime took place within these walls." Her stance, with arms crossed firmly across her undefiled bosom, indicated clearly that she would never have permitted it.

"No. We call our men Scene of Crime Officers, though – SOCO for short. It's our job to find and take away anything which might help us to discover who killed Father Bickerstaffe. You'd want to help us do that, wouldn't you?"

"There's no need to turn on the charm for me, young man." Martha could have produced nothing more charming than this last phrase for the grizzled veteran who stood awkwardly on the ancient Persian carpet in the high-ceilinged hall. "I know what has to be done. It just doesn't come easily to let someone into Father's private rooms. I've never had to do it before without his permission."

"And I trust you'll never have to do it again, I really do." Joe Jackson felt a sympathy for this upright, grieving woman, so loyal to her dead master's memory. She was one of the very few women he had come across in the last ten years who would happily have accepted the term 'master'. He leaned towards her, lapsed deliberately into the Lancashire accent he normally checked when talking to the public. "It's a rum do, this, Miss Hargreaves, and no mistake. World's coming to something, when they start murdering priests, isn't it? We'll find who did it, you know. But we'll need a lot of help from people like you."

Martha looked at him suspiciously for a moment, then nodded and unclasped her arms within their black cotton dress. She turned to the thick Victorian door behind her, which separated the hall and front room, where Father Bickerstaffe had been used to receive his callers, from the private sections of the house. "You'd best come this way, then."

She led them through to an inner hall and then up a gloomy balustraded staircase. She paused on the landing at the top of the first flight. "This is the floor where Father lived. His lounge is through here. You'll find his bedroom next door. There's a smaller bedroom next to that, for visiting clergy, and a bathroom at the end."

"And what's up those stairs?" Jackson indicated the narrower flight of stairs which ran on up to the second storey of the house.

Martha bristled a little, resisting the impulse to fold her arms back into the 'they shall not pass' position. "Those are my quarters. I trust neither you nor your staff will need to search them."

"No, indeed we shall not!" Jackson reassured her hastily. "Not at this point, anyway. But we shall need to be thorough in our search of Father Bickerstaffe's rooms. You understand that, don't you?"

"Yes. All right. I'll leave you to it, then."

"If you wouldn't mind staying, it would be useful to us, Miss Hargreaves. Quite proper, in fact. You'd be acting as a witness, you see, to anything we found. You'd be able to make sure that everything was above board."

The first smile they had seen from her surfaced at that. "Make sure you hadn't planted anything, you mean? Or 'found' anything that wasn't really here?"

"Precisely. You'd be an instrument of the law, Martha." Even his daring use of her first name passed unchecked. It was quite obvious that Martha Hargreaves, like the majority of the people they saw nowadays, had picked up all kinds of dubious notions about the police and their methods from television crime series. "Not that any member of my team would do anything that wasn't above board, of course." Joe Jackson laughed heartily at the notion, and the three people who had trailed him up the stairs laughed behind him, less heartily and quite disjointedly.

Martha watched while the three men and a woman went methodically through the big, comfortable room where Father Bickerstaffe had spent most of his leisure hours. They took the books out of the bookcase, looked carefully to see if there were any papers between them, thumbed through the books themselves for any hidden, revealing papers. They felt down the sides of the deep-seated armchairs, investigated the mahogany sideboard, lifted it out to look behind it. They went through Father's pile of CDs, took everything out of the television and video cabinet he had bought for himself last year, even lifted the ornaments on the two wide window-sills to make sure there was nothing hidden beneath them. Martha was glad that she had cleaned and dusted this room so regularly. When they had finished, Jackson nodded to the tall man in civilian clothes and he took three photographs of the room from different angles.

When they moved on to Father Bickerstaffe's bedroom, Martha's curiosity was overcome by her sense of sacrilege. Even she had rarely entered this room, for Father had insisted on making his own bed each day. She had gone in to vacuum the floor once a week and had spent no more than five minutes on each occasion in this neat, anonymous room. Now the men threw back the blankets on the bed, began to examine the sheets, then bundled them up and put them in a large plastic bag. When they opened up Father's wardrobe and began to feel through the pockets of his clothes, Martha felt she could watch them at their work no longer. "I'll away downstairs and make you some tea now," she said desperately.

The team looked at Sergeant Jackson, who after a moment's hesitation nodded and said, "We'll be down as quickly as we can, Martha. But take your time with that tea – we have to be thorough. There may just be something here that will give us a clue as to who killed Father Bickerstaffe, you see."

Martha smiled and went hastily out on to the landing. She had to brush the tears from her eyes before she could trust herself to descend the familiar gloomy staircase.

The team searched the room thoroughly, methodically, working to a system Jackson had devised through years of experience. It meant they came to the likeliest areas, the places which most people chose to hide things, at the very end of their search. And in this respect at least, Father John Bickerstaffe proved himself a conventional man. It was in the bottom drawer of his chest of drawers, beneath two pairs of underpants and a vest that had never been worn, that they found the material he had wanted to hide from the world. Pornographic material: stuff that these seasoned professionals had seen before, but which would have made poor old Martha's grey hair stand on end.

Paedophilic photographs, of the kind which are not displayed openly on newsagents' shelves even in these liberated days, but which are readily obtainable in many parts of Europe. Soft porn, by the dubious standards of the new century. Boys with old-young faces, smiling mirthless smiles, in postures scarcely conducive to laughter. The team had seen much worse, but they supposed these prints had given a sick excitement to the sad and lonely celibate who had hidden them here.

More interesting than the glossy photographs was the brief note which accompanied them. Joe Jackson picked it up deftly with his tweezers, for it might still provide fingerprints other than those of the dead man. There was no address, and the note said only, 'Thanks for the return of the magazines. Sorry to hear you don't feel able to join our little group at the moment. Let me know if you reconsider. In the meantime, you might find these pictures of passing interest. Plenty more where these came from! Yours, Chris.'

It was a casual, educated hand. A hand which had penned many words in its life. The signature was little more than a hasty scrawl, and there was no second name. Yet it was the signature that made Jackson sure that he had seen this hand before. He put the note between polythene sheets with extreme care, then made a note that it should be passed to their calligraphy expert as soon as it had been tested for prints. But in his own mind, he was already sure who had written that note.

There were times when Inspectors earned their money, he thought. He was glad that it would be that cocky little sod Percy Peach who had to follow this up.

A bright September morning with a soft breeze; white clouds moving gently across a bright blue sky; no rain since Monday, and none forecast, so the prospect of a dry round of golf on the trim acres of the North Lancs Golf Club at the weekend. All this should have made that Thursday morning a cheerful one for Percy Peach.

Yet as he got out of the police car and walked with Lucy Blake into the primary school beneath the spire of the Roman Catholic church, the Inspector was not happy. It was partly because of the child abuse which lay beneath this murder case: no policeman likes dealing with children or parents when there have been accusations of crime in this area. It was also partly because he did not know quite how he was going to tackle a primary-school headmistress. His childhood experiences of the breed, like his later experience of marriage, had left him carrying psychological baggage he would rather have been without. Percy would not of course have admitted even to possessing a subconscious, still less to any notion that it might in any way inhibit him.

The image Percy carried within him was that of a spinster, at least seventy years old in his childish eyes, acidic of expression and attitude, regarding him disapprovingly through lenses like jamjar bottoms and rapping his fingers with a ruler for the fidgeting which was his besetting sin as an eight-year-old. The headteacher who now came out from her office to meet him conformed to none of his images, and that in itself he found a little disconcerting. Mrs MacMullen was in her late forties, blond and buxom, erring a little on the side of the plumpness which most of her charges found reassuring. Hundreds of children and one or two staff had wept on her splendid bosom in the twenty years in which she had instructed the nation's young. Percy, eyeing that instrument of comfort, thought how much happier his school days might have been if such noble consolation had been available to him.

"Thank you for making time to see us," he said.

Her smile destroyed a few more of his prejudices. "It wasn't too difficult. The children aren't back at school until Monday. Most of the staff are in for in-service training, but we haven't any pupils to worry about yet. Come into the office." They followed her into a room which still had space for children's paintings on the wall in spite of the piles of books and letters which seemed to dominate it. She had both chairs and coffee ready for them, anticipating that like good police officers they would arrive precisely at the time they had appointed. She sat down opposite them in an armchair, assessing this strangely dapper little man with the bald head and jet-black moustache and the sturdy girl with the red-gold hair beside him as coolly as if they had been a pair of the anxious parents she was more used to meeting here. She said, "It must be important, to bring me a Detective Inspector and a Detective Sergeant at the same time."

"It is. And I'm not sure how much you can help us. But we do need you to be completely frank with us. We are quite sure now that we are investigating a murder."

The shrewd blue eyes widened only a little. "Then it must be that of Father Bickerstaffe."

"Yes. And we're still getting to know him. The better the picture we can get of a dead man, the better the chance that we shall locate his murderer. How well did you know Father Bickerstaffe?"

She took a few seconds to frame her answer, thinking carefully before she committed herself to words. "I knew him quite well, in what I suppose you would call a professional capacity. I don't worship at the Sacred Heart church myself – I live four miles from the school, in St Mary's parish – but John Bickerstaffe came into the school and chatted with me about our problems about once a fortnight. He was also a governor of the school. He helped to appoint me three years ago."

"I thought the parish priest controlled his local school, that he would have appointed you himself, with the approval of the local authority."

Mrs MacMullen smiled again, and once more Percy found it disconcerting. "You're years out of date, Mr Peach, I'm happy to say. May I ask if you are yourself a Catholic?"

"I – er, well, no. Not now. I was brought up as a Catholic, though."

"And your ideas of school organisation date from those days, I think. Something like that did used to happen in most Church schools, in the old days. Nowadays, the priest of the church to which the school is attached is no more than one of the governors. Father Bickerstaffe wasn't even Chair of our governing body, though he was always most helpful when it came to offering his services or providing us with accommodation for our fund-raising ventures."

Having thus been brought firmly into the new century, DI Peach nodded briefly at his sergeant, and Lucy Blake said, "We need to have your frank impressions of Father Bickerstaffe. He seems to have been killed quite deliberately and with malice aforethought. We have seen his spiritual superior, who has given us certain information. We have seen Miss Hargreaves, Father Bickerstaffe's housekeeper, who told us" – she turned here to her notebook to quote the phrases exactly – "'He was a good man . . . A kind man. Always available when there was trouble . . . Always very good when there was a death in the family . . . Thoughtful about people, understanding.' We want to know what you can add to that. And, frankly, whether you agree with all of it."

Again that pause before she replied. Lucy found herself wishing that all their interviewees would give such thought to their words before they spoke. Percy Peach, on the other hand, much preferred people to speak on impulse, because they gave away so much more of themselves that way. But then Mrs MacMullen was not one of the suspects Percy was most at home with but an innocent, intelligent woman, genuinely helping them with an enquiry. Eventually she said, "I wouldn't quarrel with any of that. Martha's a good woman, and she saw more of John Bickerstaffe than any of us. But priests are men like other men, with human weaknesses as well as virtues."

Peach, who still found it odd to hear people using the first names of priests, said, "I can't give you the detail of what Bishop Hogan told us about the situation. But it may help you to know that he indicated that Father Bickerstaffe was to be relieved of his duties as Parish Priest of the Sacred Heart."

"Yes. I suppose that was inevitable. I'm sorry it had come to that. He was a good man in so many ways. But if a man can't be trusted with children, you can't have him anywhere around them. Their only defence is the one we can give them."

They knew with these phrases not only that she knew about the priest's activities, but that she had defended the children in her school herself, against other abuses than his. Despite her comfortable appearance, Percy knew in that moment that he would not have cared to be brought into this room as an erring parent. He said, "Were there children in your school who suffered from John Bickerstaffe's actions?"

"No. Not while they were in my school. These were older children, ex-pupils of this school – aged twelve to fourteen, I think." She gave the impression that whoever had dared anything of the sort with children in her school would have had her to reckon with very quickly. But it was evident that Mrs MacMullen was in touch with both her pupils and the community around them; clearly not much would have escaped her.

"Would you agree that the abuses which went on centred around the youth club in the church hall?"

Her eyes strayed automatically to the building he mentioned. The high, windowless gable of the rear side of the hall was just visible through her window, beyond the stone wall which encircled the primary-school playground. "Yes, it seems so. The club kept a lot of children off the streets, and I like to think Father Bickerstaffe started it without any evil intentions in mind – but I don't suppose that matters now."

"No. We're not here to judge him about that, but to try to find who killed him. But what does matter is that we have full details of what was going on. That means which children were abused, and anything you know of their parents' reactions when they discovered what was happening."

There was the now familiar pause whilst she weighed the question and what her answer would be. Then she said, "Yes, I see that. I don't know any of the details of the assaults: as they were on former pupils of mine, not current ones, I didn't need details. But I'll tell you everything I know."

She gave them a series of names, a sad register of a man's sins against those least fitted to cope with his attentions. Four were the names they had collected on the previous day from their visit to the Bishop's residence. But their visit to the Sacred Heart RC Primary School was not wasted. Mrs MacMullen added a fifth name, which stopped them in their tracks for a moment. It was the name not of an abused child, but of an adult who had recently been in contact with John Bickerstaffe.

It was a name which was of immediate interest to DI Percy Peach, who knew it from another context altogether.

"Keep me fully briefed," Superintendent Tucker had ordered. As the man nominally in charge of the case, he couldn't afford not to be aware of developments. And Percy Peach was making the most of the command to relay his findings.

"We saw the Bishop yesterday, sir. Right nest of vice being built under our noses in Brunton, apparently. Lucy Blake got it out of them; once she flashed a thigh at them, they were putty in her hands." He paused to let this vision of a Lancashire Mata Hari dance into the dull brain of his superior officer. "I thought of bringing Bishop Hogan in for a bit of third degree – perhaps have him photographed with you in his robes at the station entry, I thought – but he seemed to have told us everything by the time we left."

Tucker was sure his Inspector was exaggerating. But he wasn't sure how much. He tried to force authority into his voice. "I told you to go easy. It's a delicate area. We don't want to be accused of victimising the Catholic community."

"No, sir. But they're a pretty thick lot, the Micks. Probably won't have the sense to take offence."

"Peach, that's *racialist*! Anyway, you're out of date. Only a minority of the Roman Catholic population of Lancashire are Irish nowadays."

"Irish origins, though, most of 'em. Should be grateful for what they've got. But that's between the two of us, between these four walls." Percy, who would stand for no hint of racism within his team, now tapped the side of his nose and gave Tucker the grossest of winks.

Tucker refused to be drawn further into his web. "So you think you've got all you can from the diocesan Bishop. In that case, don't visit him again without my express permission. You should be pursuing your enquiries on the ground round here. And I shouldn't need to tell you that." Tucker produced his stern look over the gold-rimmed glasses he wore when at his desk; it usually curbed lesser, more promotion-conscious men than Peach.

"Oh, but we are, sir." For a moment Percy was tempted towards genuine outrage at the suggestion that he would know so little of his duties. Then he decided Tommy Bloody Tucker was not worth his anger. "The house to house is almost complete. By the end of today, one or both parents of every member of the Sacred Heart Youth Club will have been interviewed. This morning, DS Blake and I visited Mrs MacMullen, the headmistress of the Sacred Heart Primary School, adjacent to the church. She was able to give us another name to add to those we had collected from the Bishop."

"Ah! Just one more name? You're sure she's not holding anything back? They can be clever creatures, you know, these professional women." Tucker found the workings of all female minds a foreign country, and professional women were the least accessible terrain of all.

Percy considered his chief's admonition, then allowed himself to look worried as the implications sank in. "You may be right, sir. I could bring her in here, if you like. Let you have a go at her yourself. Put her in an interview room with you and—"

"You'll do no such thing, Peach. Just be wary, that's all I'm saying." The delicious fantasy Percy had entertained for a moment of the splendidly efficient Mrs MacMullen chewing up Tommy Tucker and spitting out the pieces vanished into the air. Tucker rustled both hands through the papers on his desk and said, "Well, I've plenty to be busy with, if you haven't. Off you go and push things forward."

As he went back down the stairs, Percy reflected happily that in his agitation Tucker had omitted to force him to pass over the fifth name the headteacher had given them, which was that of a prominent local figure. He was happy about that. Keep the bugger in the ignorance he deserved, he thought.

In early September, it was dark by half-past seven. So seven o'clock was a good time to have a bonfire at the bottom of the garden. You could still see what you were about, but most people were already indoors, lamenting the summer that was almost gone and preparing for a night's television.

On this quiet evening, there was very little breeze. The plume of smoke from the tightly rolled newspapers rose almost perpendicular into the still twilight. There was not a lot of garden rubbish to burn at this time of year, but the man made a pyramid from the unplaned wood he had collected from a dismembered box. As this cone of fire crackled into life, he added the dead branches from the shrubs he had pruned after their flowering in the spring – long before he had known about any of this, he reflected grimly. That glorious spring, when the trees had dazzled with their brilliant colours and life had seemed so uncomplicated, was scarcely four months behind them. It seemed now to belong to another world.

The blaze crackled, reared up, made him leap back for a moment with the fierceness of its heat, and then burned more steadily. He saw the bed of dull red ashes that he wanted beginning to accumulate beneath the flames, as the wooden struts he had piled on end collapsed into a steady blaze. His fire was hot enough and established enough now to burn the things he wanted to destroy without leaving any trace. He turned to the plastic bag at his heels and began to extract the contents.

The handkerchief went on first, curling quickly in the heat, dissolving with a tiny flash of blue into the body of his fire. Then two cheap ball-point pens. You surely couldn't identify anyone from these, for they were far too common, but they might as well go, since there was no point in taking needless risks. He hesitated over the money. There was thirty pounds in notes, which would burn easily enough. But there was no point surely in burning anything as anonymous as money? And in any case, you couldn't burn coins. Might as well keep the notes too, then, and dispose of the lot at once; it would be a small, supplementary appendix to his revenge. But some superstition made him put this money in a separate pocket from his own, so that the two should not mix. He would get rid of it tomorrow, and have done with it. That would remove his last link with the dead man.

The three letters curled quickly in the breeze. He threw the watch in too, watching the strap writhe and burn like a live thing as the flames licked it greedily. The case might survive the flames, but there would surely be nothing identifiable left after this heat; he'd rake through and check tomorrow, to be on the safe side. He used the little diary as a test for the most important thing he had to burn. It made quite a cheerful blaze, but it did not last long. He poked a stick through the charred remnant of it, watching it flame anew, then disintegrate to nothing in the crimson heart of his fire.

He drew the last item out of the plastic bag with extreme, almost superstitious, care. It was a small, thick book with a gold cross on its black leather cover. A breviary containing the

Holy Office, extracts of which every Roman Catholic priest has to read each day, to remind him of his calling and provoke private meditation. The man held the book in both hands for a moment, then consigned it reverently to the flames, as though this was the culminating action of some religious ceremony.

It took much longer to burn than any other item and the man watched it for minutes on end without a flicker of movement, with a fascination bordering on superstition. It was not until what was left of the book dropped into the base of the embers that he made any move. The pages had now been reduced to a solid, unrecognisable black square which threatened to deaden the fire which had all but consumed them. The man chopped at this with a spade, suddenly and savagely, and watched the small back cubes he created flare again into life. Not until the last vestige of the breviary had disappeared completely and his fire was reduced to a smouldering cairn of glowing charcoal did he turn away.

It was dark now. He took a single glance back before he went into the house; all he could see of his work were faintly glowing embers through the early night. His last connections with Father John Bickerstaffe had been destroyed.

Seven

Peach, driving out alone into the lush green countryside of the Ribble Valley on a beautiful September morning, would have liked to have had Lucy Blake at his side to chat to; he felt easier with her now than he had felt for a long time with any woman. But she could be better employed elsewhere. Besides, he was going to a place designed for men and run by men; they might just feel it easier to be completely open with him if he didn't have a sparky young woman at his side.

Downton Hall, the place where he now presumed John Bickerstaffe had spent his last troubled nights on this earth, was beautifully set at the head of a gently sloping valley, in the foothills of the northern Pennines. Pendle Hill, with its abrupt Western profile and its associations with the Lancashire witches, was a few miles to the south of it, its greater bulk cutting off the mansion from the last of the sizeable Lancashire industrial towns, Burnley, Preston and his own base, Brunton.

The Hall was a solid stone building, built towards the end of the nineteenth century, when King Cotton ruled the back-to-back streets of brick houses in the Lancashire towns and his courtiers built themselves places like this for weekends and holidays. It had been a legacy to the church when death duties threatened in the days after the 1939–45 war. It had become a place for older priests to live out their last days and younger ones to enjoy a holiday away from the demands of their insistent parishes. And a place for those who transgressed to be hidden, whilst the hierarchy of the church decided what should be done with them, Percy Peach thought, as he drove between the high gateposts and up the long drive.

He had got here more quickly than he expected on the A59, a faster and very different road from the one he had cycled during his youth to reach the Yorkshire Dales. It was barely twenty past nine when he found himself sitting in the cool and rather musty room by the front door which was used for the reception of all visitors. Through the wide stone-framed bay window, he could see the broad swathes of pink-cerise heather on the fells, clear in the morning sun as the land climbed away towards the Trough of Bowland. It wasn't more than three miles from this place to the spot where the body had been discovered, Peach computed. Bickerstaffe could have walked there, probably had. No chance of significant detail about times and his state of mind from a helpful driver, then. Still less of any clue as to whom he might have met. But you couldn't anticipate what you would find in places like this; you had to keep alert, keep trying, and hope for the unexpected.

His doleful thoughts were interrupted by the arrival of Monsignor Eaton, a silver-haired, urbane cleric who had himself been put out to grass in this place when he reached the age of seventy. He was still lean and erect as he hurried into the room and apologised for keeping his visitor waiting. "Been down to our little church in Downton to say Mass," he explained. "First Friday, you know. Country people are busy at this time of the year, but we still get quite a little gathering on First Fridays."

Peach was at a loss for a moment. Then he remembered from

his youth that there was some custom that if you made a good Communion (whatever that was) on the first Friday of nine successive months, you could be assured that your immortal soul would not go to hell. Some saint had told people it was so, on the strength of a vision or something equally unlikely – Percy couldn't remember the details. He smiled weakly and said, "It's not your fault, Father. I was early." 'Monsignor' was too much of a mouthful for him, and the cultivated figure before him didn't register any annoyance at the lower title.

With commendable directness, the old priest said, "I understand you want to talk to me about poor Father Bickerstaffe. I shan't be able to tell you much. I think you know the circumstances under which he came here."

"I do. Had the Church decided what it was going to do with him?"

Monsignor Eaton smiled. "In two thousand years, the church has had to learn to deal with the weaknesses, even the vices, of its servants. In the context of medieval popes, Father Bickerstaffe's sins would hardly have rated a headline. That does not mean they were not serious, especially for those who suffered at his hands. But people like him are sent here first and foremost to remove them from the places where they have erred. After that, the problem is not so much what the church will do with them so much as what they will do with themselves. They come here to contemplate what they have done, to see it from a distance, and then to decide what they should do with the rest of their lives."

"But they are offered guidance about that, surely?"

"They are. But as far as possible, we prefer that they ask for that guidance, rather than having it compelled upon them."

"I see. And did Father Bickerstaffe ask for such guidance?"

"He did not. But he was only here for a few days before

– before he disappeared. I had a few words with him on the first day he came here, because he was in a highly emotional state. He seemed very near to what for us is the worst sin of all, Despair, and I told him that we were here to offer help, not to judge him."

"And what was his reaction?"

There was a slight shrug of Monsignor Eaton's aged but still elegant shoulders. "John knew as well as I do that one can't deny the infinite mercy of God. He quietened down a little and agreed to speak to me when he had been here for a while. He was quiet on the following days, but I think he was coming to terms with himself. He walked a lot on the fells. This is an ideal place for fresh air and contemplation, Inspector."

That's true. Perhaps I should try it myself, thought Percy, instead of just meaning to. I could walk these hills and valleys with Lucy; I'd enjoy that. He said, "Could you show me the room which Father Bickerstaffe occupied when he was here?"

It was a cell-like room in the upper part of the house. Comfortable enough, but simple. It was long and narrow, confirming Peach's view that it was a larger room which had been divided since the days when this was a private residence. A small crucifix and a view of St Peter's in Rome were the only things adorning the blue-emulsioned walls. The room had a striking view through its single window, looking north towards the distant heights of Ingleborough and Pen-Y-Ghent. The only habitation he could see was a distant farmhouse, the only moving life visible that of a few sheep on the hillside beyond it. A good place for contemplation, this.

Without looking back from this view, Peach said quietly, "How many people knew he had come here, Father?"

"Impossible to say. We don't make any public announcement, as you'd expect. But Father Bickerstaffe could have told people – I don't know whether he did or not. Probably his housekeeper would know, if he wanted his mail forwarded."

"But it wouldn't have been too difficult for anyone who wanted to know where he'd gone to find out he was here?"

"No, I'm sure it wouldn't. People gossip around a parish, as they do anywhere else, and I'm afraid there's more interest once there's a breath of scandal. People could even have guessed where he'd gone. Most Catholics in the diocese know of the existence of this place; it wouldn't take a lot of intelligence to make an informed guess that this is where he was."

"You haven't touched anything here?"

"No. The room hasn't been needed, so in view of the circumstances we didn't disturb things. It was cleaned on the day after he disappeared and the sheets were changed – we didn't know then that anything had happened to him, of course."

Those old enemies of forensic science, the cleaners and the launderers. In this case, Peach doubted whether they had destroyed anything of value. He looked through the room's sparse furnishings. There was a single clean shirt in the top drawer of the chest, two pairs of socks and a pair of underpants in the one beneath it. A cassock depended from a hanger in the wardrobe, looking at once sinister and pathetic. He wondered if the dead man had considered whether he would ever put it on again. An electric shaver and a brush and comb were on the shelf over the washbasin beyond the bed. No letters; no books, save for a copy of a thriller with a bookmark at page 197.

Peach said, "Help me, Father. Is there anything missing which you would expect to be here?"

"I think he received at least one letter whilst he was here. He could have discarded that, of course. But there is one thing a priest is never without: his breviary. Every priest has to read the appropriate section of the Holy Office every day."

"Forgive me for the suggestion, but is it possible that Father Bickerstaffe had discarded his breviary? He was clearly severely disturbed, and we don't know how he thought of his future."

Monsignor Eaton shook his grey, experienced head. "I don't think so. Reading the Holy Office daily is a habit bred into us over the years. He'd have needed to be very disturbed to break that habit – from what little I saw of him I judge it would have been one of his few consolations. Even if I'm wrong about that, I'm sure he'd never have destroyed or discarded the book itself. But he probably took it out on his walks with him – I'd like to think it was a source of comfort for him in his desolation."

Peach nodded. "There was nothing at all in his pockets when his body was found. That means they were almost certainly emptied by whoever killed him. If we could find that book, we might find his killer with it. But I doubt whether we ever shall. Is there anyone at the house whom Father Bickerstaffe talked to whilst he was staying with you?"

"Just one person. I know they talked together two or three times in the days before he disappeared. I've asked him to stand by to meet you. It's a Father Irwin. He should be waiting for you in my office downstairs."

Monsignor Eaton took him down the wide mahogany stair-case, showed him the room and discreetly withdrew. A man in his mid-thirties, short and stocky in an open-necked shirt and a well-worn tweed jacket, sprang up swiftly when Peach went into the room, and Percy divined that he had been waiting nervously within it for some time. When he introduced himself, the man said, "No 'Father' any more for me, please. I'm to be plain Denis Irwin from now on, so I might as well get used to it sooner rather than later."

"Very well. Denis it is. I gather that you chatted a little with Father Bickerstaffe before he disappeared. You know he's been murdered?"

"Yes. I heard it on the radio in my room. It was a tremendous shock, I can tell you."

"It must have been. When did you last see him?"

"On the afternoon of the day he disappeared. That was Thursday the twentieth of August – a fortnight ago yesterday." Irwin had the intense air of a man who had been over this many times in his own mind.

"Do you remember the time?"

"Yes. It was late in the afternoon, almost five o'clock, I think."

"And did he give you any indication where he was going?"

"I didn't speak to him, I'm afraid. I just saw him going off down the drive. You can see it from the window of my room. I remember thinking it was late for him to be starting one of his walks. He went for long walks on the fells, you know, tramped for miles and miles on his own."

"Perhaps he was going out to meet someone."

"Yes. I've thought of that since, in view of what's happened. It didn't strike me as a possibility at the time, but it would explain why he was going out so late in the day."

"If he was going to meet someone, have you any idea who it might have been?"

"No. We talked a bit, but you couldn't call us intimates. We were partners in distress, if you like. We exchanged notes about our problems. John told me what he'd done. It helped me, because it made my problems seem manageable. I'm leaving

78

the priesthood, Mr Peach: I realise now that I should never have been a celibate. I shall be marrying a lady from my parish, once I find out how I'm going to make a living."

He had the gathering confidence of a man who had made a difficult decision, combined with the bright enthusiasm of an adolescent in love. Percy Peach found it a most irritating combination. Silly bugger wants me to ask him about this woman and his own scandal, he thought. Instead he said, "Good for you, Denis Irwin. Now, can we get back to Father Bickerstaffe? I'm trying to find out who killed him – I take it he didn't seem to you like a potential suicide?"

"No. He was very shaken, but I think he still saw himself as a priest. I don't think taking his own life would have been an option for John."

"Right. Think carefully. You're my last link with a dead man. Do you know if anyone contacted him while he was here?"

Denis Irwin forced himself to think back carefully, however much he would have liked to air his own problems with a neutral listener. "No one came here to see him, I'm sure of that. He had a letter, the day after he came, because he opened it while we were having breakfast, and it upset him. He crumpled it up and put it in his pocket quickly, without finishing reading it, I think, and he looked quite distressed."

"Any phone calls?"

"Yes. Two at least. He told me he'd had one the first day. Threatening him with violence, he said, if he did what he was going to do. I think it was the same person or persons who'd sent the letter which had so upset him, but I couldn't be sure. Anyway, he said it wouldn't stop him, that this was some good he could do, whatever the damage he'd done. I didn't know what he was talking about and I didn't ask him. He seemed far too upset at the time, and I thought then that there'd be other opportunities in the days to come, if he wanted to discuss it with me." He sighed bleakly at the thought of how abruptly their discussions had been terminated.

Peach said, "So we only have his own word that this call actually took place. But you mentioned two calls."

"Yes. I know a little more about the second one, because I was indirectly involved. There's a phone in the hall outside what we call the common room. I know John had at least that call when he was here, because I had to go and get him from his room to answer it."

"When was this?"

"On the night before he disappeared." The priest's rather flat features suddenly lit up with alarm. "Do you think someone was arranging to meet him the next evening?"

Percy controlled his irritation with this thirty-five-year-old who seemed to have been so protected from some aspects of life. "It seems like a possibility, doesn't it? It may even have been the person he said had already threatened him. You say you took the call. At what time on that Wednesday evening?"

"It must have been at about quarter to eight. I was watching *Coronation Street*, I have to confess. I used to pretend it kept me in touch with my congregation, but if I'm honest I have to confess—"

"Was it a man or a woman?"

"A woman. Yes, I'm pretty sure it was a woman. She didn't say much, but—"

"Can you remember anything distinctive about the voice? It's important: it must be obvious to you now that this might have been the person who killed your friend John Bickerstaffe. Or perhaps the person who set him up to be killed."

The squat face filled with a mixture of horror and excitement, a familiar combination for Peach. Innocents drawn into murder enquiries almost invariably felt the unexpected glamour of the simplest and gravest of all crimes. There was disappointment in Irwin's voice as he eventually said, "No. The voice just asked if Father John Bickerstaffe was there and I said I would go and get him."

"How long was Father Bickerstaffe on the phone?"

"Not long. Perhaps two minutes at most."

"And did he seem agitated after the call?"

"I didn't see him, I'm afraid. He didn't come into the common room. He must have gone straight back up to his room. I saw him the next morning at breakfast, and again at lunch. He seemed very quiet, now that I look back at it, but I thought he was just wrestling with his problems and he'd talk to me when he wanted to. Those would be the last times when we actually spoke." He seemed suddenly, belatedly, on the edge of tears with that thought.

Peach drove from Downton Hall back to the place where the body had been found. The stream which had been in such spate at that time was quiet now, running softly under the old stone bridge towards the spire of the village church a few hundred yards below it, contributing the soft note of water over pebbles to the village idyll.

He had a more accurate time for the murder, and the place had probably been somewhere near here. How, when and where were almost established now. It was high time to set about finding out who and why.

While Peach was pursuing his enquiries at Downton Hall, Detective Sergeant Lucy Blake was visiting a very different house. She was in one of the back-to-back terraces which the

81

original occupants of that country mansion had built for their workers in Brunton.

The worst of these, the ones with only a shared toilet or a brick cube 'petty' at the bottom of the yard, had been cleared in the optimistic housing programmes of the sixties and seventies. But the slightly better terraces, or those in 'respectable' parts of the old cotton-weaving town, had survived until refurbishment rather than clearance became the housing buzz-word. It was one of these areas that Lucy now visited, sandwiched between the canal and the old road to Preston: a quiet section of the town, a little run-down perhaps, and with more than its due share of older people who had refused to move out with the passing years. There were good small houses within these streets, houses which had had money spent on them; houses which were trim and well kept without and comfortable within; 'little palaces' in the sentimental hyperbole of those who sang their virtues.

Number Eight Primrose Bank was no palace. You stepped straight into the living room from the street, and the paper on the walls had probably been there for a good fifteen years. The three-piece suite was battered, the table under the window scratched. The print of charging elephants which was the sole wall decoration looked ill-chosen rather than exotic. Lucy sniffed the air apprehensively as she followed the woman into the house. But there was no unpleasant smell: the house had passed the police officer's first test. Police personnel, like social workers and district nurses, have to go into all kinds of habitations. The smell is their first fear, as any PC who has had to break in to discover a week-old corpse will testify.

The woman had a grey skirt and a dark green sweater, well worn but clean. She was without rings or earrings; a single pewter brooch was the only gesture towards jewellery, and her long pale face had no make-up. Her dark hair was cut quite short, with a single slide at the crown of her head. Her grey eyes were alert and watchful.

Lucy said formally, "You are Mrs Katherine Maxted?"

"Kate Maxted, yes. I'm not too keen on the Mrs, and I haven't been called Katherine since I was four and my gran died."

"Kate, then. You're divorced?"

"Not yet. Very soon, I hope. He wouldn't co-operate – he'd have to pay proper maintenance, wouldn't he? And regularly. But I should have my divorce in the next month or two, if the bloody lawyers can be persuaded to get their fingers out." The words were bitter, but there was little animation in her expression of them. Her monotone indicated that she had explained this many times before, in many different contexts.

"You live here as the only adult?" You didn't mention men or women nowadays, any more than colour.

"Yes. I rent the place, or the state rents it for me."

There had been a hesitation before she spoke, as if she were working out what it was best to say. When you lived 'on the social', you grew used to being cautious about what you revealed of your domestic circumstances. Lucy watched her steadily, without embarrassment. Peach had taught her among other things that a steady scrutiny of interviewees and an absence of the small talk with which most people greased the wheels of social exchange could sometimes unnerve people. Peach liked to see them unnerved, and Lucy could understand why when she considered some of the results. "And you have the four children of your marriage living here with you?"

"You know I have. I told all this to the woman in uniform who came yesterday. To save you checking on your homework,

83

they're aged fourteen, eleven, eight and seven. We were supposed to stop at two, but drink weakens resolution, they tell me. Wish they'd told me in time." It was all said without rancour, as a series of simple statements of fact, in the same monotone she had used earlier. Lucy began to wonder if there were drugs anywhere in the house's meagre furnishings; she was becoming more expert in recognising the symptoms of dependency, simply through experience. But it might be no more than a weary apathy about her situation which the woman was projecting. The only adornments to the room which were at all personal were group and individual photographs of the four children.

Lucy said evenly, "You must bear with me if I check these things, Mrs Maxted. I'm not checking on what you tell the social services. I'm here in connection with a very serious crime. The most serious of all, in fact."

"Aye. Murder. Friar Fucking Tuck. Father Fucking Bickerstaffe, the Flashing Friar. I just wish he'd flashed at me, that's all. I'd have cut it off for him!"

The anger was startling in its suddenness after the apathy before it. It wasn't an unusual attitude where sexual offences were concerned, and it didn't shock Lucy, as Kate Maxted had obviously hoped it might. She was glad, indeed, to see some spirit and emotion back in the woman's speech and attitude. "I'm told he assaulted your son. Is that correct?"

"Yes. Wayne. Bloody stupid name, isn't it? But that was his father all over. Called him after some American cowboy and hoped he'd grow up thumping everyone in sight. That was Dermot all over. But you get used to a name, in time, and it doesn't matter." It was the first time she had mentioned her husband's name. She was suddenly anxious. "Here, you won't want to interview Wayne again, will you? He spoke to some priest and another bloke about it a couple of months ago. Upset him quite enough, that did."

"There shouldn't be any need for that at this stage. But whatever you thought of Father Bickerstaffe, he's been murdered. And it's our job to find out who killed him."

"Aye, a team of thirty, it said in the *Evening Telegraph*. Pity you didn't put that number on to controlling his bloody antics when he were alive."

But it was no more than the ritual complaint of the wronged, the parent bitter on behalf of a child. She was calm again now, even watchful. Lucy said quietly, "We'd have investigated it, if anyone had reported it at the time. Brought a prosecution, once we found it was justified and we had the evidence."

"Aye. Well, it's not my fault you hadn't. If the lad had only talked at the time, you'd have known fast enough."

"Yes, I believe that, Kate. You shouldn't be surprised that Wayne didn't tell you, though. Children don't know how to deal with these things, so they just bottle them up and don't tell anyone until they're forced to speak."

The woman looked at her quickly, as if she was checking that she was not being patronised. "That's how Wayne was. One minute sullen as hell, the next in tears with his arms round my neck." She was silent, savouring the moment when her teenager had suddenly been as close and dependent as a four-year-old again, whatever the dark reason for it.

"Whatever Father Bickerstaffe did – and I can assure you there are people who've done much worse things with children – no one had any right to murder him. We shall find out who did it, in due course." Lucy hoped she sounded more confident than she felt at that moment.

Kate Maxted nodded. "I know that. Just don't expect *me* to shed any tears over the bastard, that's all. I'm not stupid, you know. Left school with six O levels, I did. Could have gone on for A levels and university, they said. Wish I had: at least I'd have avoided marrying Dermot Bloody Maxted if I'd done that."

"Is your husband still in touch with the children, Kate?"

"No, he bloody isn't. Not so much as a birthday card for any of them." She looked up suddenly at DS Blake as she realised the reason for the question. "So if you think he might have come riding back like John Bloody Wayne to avenge his son, you're mistaken. Doubt if he even knew what Friar Tuck had done to him, 'cos I didn't tell him. Haven't even spoken to him, this last three or four months."

Lucy wondered if something or someone had arrived to divert her in those months. Wouldn't the normal expression have been simply 'for three or four months'? The team would need to investigate any liaison she was concealing, in due course. They didn't know, perhaps never would know, the exact circumstances of this killing, but it could well have been easier for two people than for one to plan it and execute it. She said quietly, "It looks as though we can at least eliminate Mr Maxted from suspicion of murder, then."

"Aye, that's Dermot all over. Never around when the shit begins to fly. You can take it from me he's no idea what's happened to his own son, let alone to the sky pilot who abused him." Discovering the crumpled paper from a Mars Bar down the side of her armchair, she flung it savagely into the empty fireplace, as if the action could relieve some of her resentment against this absentee father.

Lucy Blake made her first written note during the exchange. They could ignore Dermot Maxted in their investigation, unless he proved part of a larger conspiracy. She said, deliberately low-key, "How did you find out what had been happening to Wayne, Kate?"

"He didn't tell me. Looking back, I can see that he came home upset from that youth club at the Sacred Heart once or twice, but I thought it was just adolescence – probably girl trouble, I remember thinking at the time." She smiled bitterly at the recollection of her mistake. "It wasn't until this priest and a bloke he said was a psychiatrist came round here and said they wanted to talk to Wayne that I knew there was anything serious. Apparently another boy had mentioned his name. At first I thought Wayne had done something wrong, but I soon realised what had been going on."

"And did you go to see Father Bickerstaffe yourself?"

"No. The priest who came asked me not to – said the diocese was going to deal with it, that he'd be back to see me again in due course to tell me what had happened to Bickerstaffe. He gave me the impression that there might be some money in it for us if we kept quiet: the other man said they'd have to discuss what compensation might be appropriate. But that wouldn't have stopped me going to see the bastard. Only they whipped him away, didn't they? He was gone before I could get to him – on the day after they'd been to see me, apparently."

"Probably just as well. It wouldn't have done you any good to see him, believe me. These things are best left to the law."

"You mustn't take the law into your own hands, you mean? That's what people said to me at the time. But it wasn't their kid who'd been assaulted, was it? Anyway, some bugger did take the law into his own hands, and saw the bastard off. And good luck to him, I say." Her jaw jutted forward to emphasise her vehemence, challenging her listener to deny her.

Instead, Lucy said quietly, "Why do you say 'he', Kate?

Have you some reason to believe that it might have been a man who did this?"

For the first time, fear flashed across Kate Maxted's pale face; it was there only for an instant before it gave way to puzzlement, but it made Lucy wonder if the woman had something to hide. Kate said carefully, "No, of course not. I just assumed it would have been a man. It usually is, isn't it, when there's violence about?"

Now she was appealing to the sorority against men, when a moment ago she had been approving that very violence herself. But you couldn't often expect logic from the public once emotions were involved, and still less from the mother of an abused child. Lucy smiled back at the intense face. "More often than not it is men, yes, when violence is involved. But we know from the cause of death that this killing could have been by a woman, so we have to keep an open mind."

Apprehension stole back into Kate Maxted's sallow features. "You mean you've got me in the frame, don't you? You mean I could have found the bastard and seen him off."

"I mean we would like to eliminate you from our enquiries, that's all. Just as you have yourself eliminated your husband, Dermot. So that we can concentrate on the people who might really have done this. I need you to tell me where you were on Thursday the twentieth and Friday the twenty-first of August."

A slight pause, then an unexpected smile. "You don't know just when he died, do you? You're going to find it difficult to pin anyone down if you don't know any better than that when he was killed." She didn't disguise her satisfaction in the thought.

It was disconcerting when people spotted the weaknesses of which only police personnel should be aware. Lucy tried not to be nettled. "Just tell me where you were, Kate, and let us do the detecting." At that very moment, had she but known it, DI Peach was pinning the probable time of the murder down to late on Thursday.

Kate Maxted looked for a moment as if she would refuse an answer. Then she thought better of it and said, "It's a fortnight and more ago, you know. When the kids are on holiday from school, one day's much the same as another. I think I was here with the kids on the Friday. Might have gone to the shops in the morning, but I do know I was here at tea-time, because I gave them cottage pie – the young ones like that. Thursday Wayne was playing cricket – he's pretty good, they tell me. He was picked for the county boys. They played on the East Lancs ground, and my mother took the other kids up to watch him in the afternoon, and then back to her house for their tea."

"And where were you that day?"

"I was here. Putting my feet up. Watching an old video a mate lent me. *The Piano*. Not the kind of thing you can watch with kids around, I can tell you. They have a low boredom threshold where romance is concerned."

Alone then, and free of the kids, on the Thursday. Lucy made another note. "I have to ask you formally, Kate: have you any idea who killed Father John Bickerstaffe?"

"No. I might not tell you if I did know, but fortunately I haven't a clue."

"All right. We may need to speak to you again in due course. In the meantime, if you think of anything which may help us to arrest a murderer, you must remember that it is your duty to report it to us immediately."

She held Kate Maxted's eye as they both rose to their feet. The woman looked for a moment as if she would protest, would deny any obligation to help the police in this. Then she nodded abruptly and opened the single door to the street outside.

She stood in the doorway, watching the police car until Lucy Blake drove round the corner at the bottom of the street and disappeared. In the silence which followed, she could hear the high-pitched excitement of children enjoying their morning break in the playground of the primary school three streets away. She turned back into the house, shut the door, and went to the phone in the kitchen beyond the living room.

"The police have been again. CID this time . . . No, a woman. Detective Sergeant, I think she said she was . . . No. She asked a lot of questions, but I didn't tell her about us. If she speaks to the kids she'll find out though, won't she? . . . No, perhaps not. They don't seem to know just when he died, which is something . . . I suppose you're right. But come whenever you can. I need you. You know that."

Martha Hargreaves was finding it difficult to adjust to living in a presbytery without a priest.

Her life had been built for so long upon service that she felt guilty when she had no one to serve. She told herself to treat this time between priests as a holiday. That worked for about a day and a half. Then she began to feel guilty again. She cleaned the rooms which did not need cleaning. But she could not cook for a man who was not there, and her own meals seemed hardly worth the trouble she had taken for so long over those of others.

So when at nine o'clock on Friday night there came a ringing at the door of the presbytery, she hurried cheerfully to open it. It must be at the least a parishioner with some parish task for her. It might even be the canon from St Peter's with news of a new priest to follow poor Father Bickerstaffe.

It was neither of these. It was a man with a long coat, a woollen hat, and a scarf wrapped about his face. He reminded Martha of the rebels she had seen in Sean O'Casey plays, when the church dramatic society had put on daring productions some years earlier. She could only see his eyes as he said gruffly, "Father Bickerstaffe had some papers for me. I'm to come in and get them from his rooms."

He made to push past her, but Martha barred his way, surprising him. The modern church housekeeper has had to get used to being firm with those who think church houses an easy touch for their depredations. "Father's gone away. Who are you?"

The man was impatient with her delay. "I know he's gone away, woman. I know he's dead. But there's things in his room he'd left there for me. Things he'd want me to have."

"What things? If you describe them to me, I'll look for them, and perhaps you can have them tomorrow. You're not coming into this house tonight." Martha stood with arms folded on the step above him, an ageing Joan of Arc protecting the Lord's servant and his house.

"You wouldn't know, woman. I'll need to see them for myself. It won't take me five minutes."

"It won't take you any minutes, because you're not coming in here. Anyway, there's nothing left in Father's rooms to interest you. The police have taken everything away." Though she had spent all her life in Lancashire, she pronounced 'police' in the Irish way, with a long 'o', as her mother had always done.

Martha was scared, despite her resolution that he should not pass, for the front door of the presbytery after dark was an isolated place, invisible from the road. But apparently she had said the right thing with the mention of the police, for the man recoiled a step from her. "When was this?"

"Two days ago. Last Wednesday." She sensed the strength the news was giving her. "Four of them, there were. A Scene of Crime team." She brought out the phrase triumphantly.

"Did they take much away?"

Martha didn't know. But she knew now how to repel this man. "Lots of things. Everything that might help them to find out who had had dealings with Father Bickerstaffe, they said. I should try Brunton Police Station, if I were you."

She watched the man's disappearance between the blackened stone gateposts with considerable satisfaction, then took her pounding heart back indoors. She pressed the big bolt which had not been used for years across the door before she went into her warm kitchen to make a cup of tea. While the kettle was boiling, she rang the police station to tell them about her caller.

Eight

Charles Courcey pushed back his immaculate white cuff and looked at his watch. Twenty to twelve. In twenty minutes it would be over again for another month.

Many of his Parliamentary colleagues paid lip service to the clinic in the constituency as a valuable part of an MP's duties. Kept them in touch with their voters, they said. Proved to their constituents that they had a real link with the Parliament that often seemed so distant and so faceless. Some of the masochists even held them once a week.

Once a month was quite enough for Charles Courcey, though his Press releases always said once a fortnight. Only made the buggers moan more, if you gave them too many opportunities for complaint, in his view. And some of the most consistent complainers hadn't even voted for him. Some of the people who contacted him here even had the face to tell him they hadn't voted for him. Charles always said that was an example of real democracy at work, of a member representing not a section but all of his constituents. But behind his wide smile there was an irritation that pathetic people like this should have the cheek to ask for his help.

An old woman came in now to ask if her dying husband could have the medals he thought he was entitled to from his service in Crete in World War II. He promised to investigate and let her know: ten minutes' work for his secretary on Tuesday. A couple wanted his help against a council who had passed a neighbour's plans for a two-storey extension which would take away much of their light. He diverted them expertly into writing to the next bureaucrat in the stages of planning appeal. It was three minutes to twelve and he was fastening up his case when a dapper little bald man with a black moustache came bouncing into his room.

"You're rather late, I'm afraid. We finish at twelve and I have another appointment, you see. If it's a quick one, I might just squeeze you in, I suppose. What is it that's troubling you?" Charles switched to his polite but brisk mode and forced a smile on to his broad lips.

The short man regarded him aggressively, without according him any immediate reply. He sat down uninvited in the chair opposite the MP. Then, as if it were an afterthought, he produced his warrant card and held it a foot from the florid face opposite him. "There are a lot of things troubling me, sir. But probably only one that you can help me with. How long it takes depends on you. You are, I presume, Charles Courcey, MP for the Hodder Valley?"

Charles decided on the hauteur he normally found effective with London policemen. "I have the pleasure of being your honourable member, yes. Now—"

"Not mine, sir. I'm from Brunton, you see. We're Labour there. Not that it would make any difference to this if you were Monster Raving Loony."

"I see. Well, I am indeed Charles Courcey. In fact, if you want to be totally pedantic –" the honourable MP looked as if he expected Peach to be just that "– the old family name is 'de Courcey', but in these egalitarian days I thought a simple

Courcey would be enough. Don't want to gather votes from simple snobbery, do we?"

"Don't we, sir? Well, I don't claim to know a lot about politics. I understood it was your father who dropped the 'de' after the bankruptcy, when he started to trade again, but it really doesn't matter now. Of course, if it comes to an arrest, we like to have the name exactly right. And my name is Peach, sir, Detective Inspector Peach, if you want to be totally pedantic."

Courcey licked thick lips, which had abruptly ceased to smile. "You're saying you want to talk to me about a police matter? Well, it goes without saying that I shall be anxious to give you whatever help I can. But I don't see that there will be very much I can do for you. Er, what is it that . . . ?"

The muscular, aggressive figure had interrupted him previously. Now, when he expected to be cut short, Peach let him wander on, until his syntax and his words petered out. He regarded Courcey steadily for a moment. Then, without taking his eyes from the increasingly disconcerted face, he called over his shoulder, "Come in here and shut the door, DS Blake, will you?"

A young woman with rich red-gold hair appeared as suddenly as the Inspector had done, closed the door unhurriedly and placed a chair alongside that of Peach. She drew a notebook and a small gold ball-point from her shoulder bag and regarded the heavily built man on the other side of the desk as calmly and unblinkingly as her Inspector.

Courcey had been glad to see that the Detective Sergeant was a woman. He had a vague feeling which probably went back to his public school days that a female presence would be softer and more accommodating, making this odd situation malleable, when he had decided how he wished to shape it. He was deprived of that comfort before Lucy Blake even spoke, for he found the shut door and the four eyes fixed so watchfully upon him quite unnerving. Peach eventually said calmly, "We are investigating the murder of a Father John Bickerstaffe, Parish Priest of the Sacred Heart Church in Brunton."

Courcey licked his too-mobile lips, tried to imagine himself putting a point in one of the House Committees, where everyone said he was quite effective. "Then I fail to see how I can help you, Inspector. I'm not a Roman Catholic myself, and Brunton as you know is not part of my constituency. I don't think I've ever visited the church – the Church of the Sacred Heart, did you say it was? I'm sorry this poor fellow has been murdered, but I really don't see how I can be of any assistance in your investigation . . ."

Peach had used that trick again, he realised: let him ramble on with his futile justifications, becoming ever less sure of his ground as he waited for the interruption that did not come. The Inspector now lifted the black business briefcase he carried and set it on the very edge of the big desk which separated the two men. He opened the lid, positioning it carefully so that it obscured the MP's view of what he was extracting. Peach looked at the single sheet of paper for a moment himself, while Courcey grew increasingly anxious. Not until the MP fancied he could hear his own heart beating did Peach pass the sheet across the desk to him. Courcey was conscious of Peach's fingernails, unexpectedly spotless and well groomed, as he took the sheet and tried to stop the trembling of his own hands. Like a lawyer completing a necessary formality, the Inspector said, "Would you confirm for me that this is your writing, sir?"

'Thanks for the return of the magazines. Sorry to hear you don't feel able to join our little group at the moment. Let me

know if you reconsider. In the meantime, you might find these pictures of passing interest . . .'

The rest of the words dissolved into dancing hieroglyphics before Courcey's horrified eyes. He strove to find his voice, to steady his pulse, before he looked up to face the four eyes he knew would be studying his reaction to this. He found he could not face these people down. He remained looking at the desk, forcing himself to concentrate fiercely upon his words, as he said, "This is just a short note, so I couldn't be sure. I write a lot of notes, you know, in my job. And I . . . I don't recognise the content. Not at all."

"The calligraphy experts seem quite certain this is your hand, sir. One of our sergeants had a note from you, you see, scribbled on the end of a letter from the Minister for Social Services when he asked you to help with the rehousing of his mother. Apparently the word 'Sorry' and the 'Yours' at the end were almost identical in the two samples."

"Well, I've never put much faith in these so-called hand-writing experts myself, and if that's all they can find to—"

"Oh, I agree with you there, sir. They seem to presume a lot from a few simple strokes." Percy allowed himself his first smile since he had entered the room, its effect the more dazzling because it was so unexpected. As swiftly as it had arrived, it was replaced by a look of concern. "But the courts do seem to place a lot of reliance on them, these days. And our calligraphy lady is apparently one of the most reputable." He noted with delight the nervous flick of apprehension which twitched the heavy eyebrows of his subject with the mention of court. He'd had more reaction from this decadent bugger than you got from many a teenage yobbo nowadays, he thought happily. He hadn't lost his timing.

Courcey looked up at him for the first time in two minutes.

"This is signed 'Chris'," he said. He pushed the note back across the table. "Quite clearly, if you look at it."

Peach did not. He said, "I noted that, sir. I also noted in our station copy of *Who's Who* that your third name is Christopher. Charles Walter Christopher Courcey, if I remember right." He rolled the names around his mouth as if savouring a fine wine.

Courcey said dully, "But I never use the Christopher."

"Not in your public duties or pronouncements, no, sir. But in your private activities, those you would very much like to prevent from becoming public, it seems that you prefer to use this other name." He put the paper back into his case, so carefully that his action clearly suggested that it might in due course become Exhibit A in some criminal court.

Courcey tried not to watch the lid of the briefcase closing on his future. He tried bluster. "Now look here, Inspector whatever-your-name-is—"

"No! You look here, Mr Courcey." Peach's voice cut like a whip across his opponent's face. It was the first time he had raised it since he had appeared so suddenly in the room. "I believe that you wrote this note. I also believe that you sent with it photographs which could lead to a prosecution under the Obscene Materials Law. I also believe that you sent someone to attempt to retrieve these materials from the presbytery of the Sacred Heart Church in Brunton last night, because you hoped they still might be found there. You're in no position to dictate to me, Mr Courcey, so I suggest you do not add threatening a police officer to your other offences."

Peach gave a tiny nod to the woman at his side. She watched the MP as his world began to collapse around him. He had always seemed a large-framed, jovial figure when

he appeared on television or in person to make public pronouncements. Now that frame seemed to grow visibly smaller
as the shoulders slumped forward. She said quietly, "I think
it's likely that other police officers will want to speak to you in
due course, Mr Courcey. Paedophilia is a serious crime, and the
law about photographs of children is still quite explicit. They
will want details of the membership of the ring into which
you tried to draw Father Bickerstaffe, and an account of its
activities. This morning, Inspector Peach and I are concerned
with a murder investigation. We have reason to believe that
you threatened Father Bickerstaffe. You can see why that must
interest us."

He looked at her with wide, sad eyes for a moment, as if
he could not believe that an attractive woman would say such
things to him. Perhaps with his tastes, thought Peach, the last
woman he had been close to was the school matron. For a
moment, it looked as though Courcey would try to bludgeon
them with words again. Then he shrugged wearily and said,
"He wouldn't join us. He was just a Holy Joe with a weakness
for stroking boys. I realised that, when it was too late. We had
thought he might give us access to his youth club, you see,
but he drew back at that. I should never have sent him the
photographs."

He was weary now, near to tears, bowed down by his
self-pity, looking in vain for some way out of this. Peach
savoured his despair for a moment; paedophiles never touched
the chord of sympathy in him which he occasionally felt
with other criminals. Eventually he said, "Did you kill John
Bickerstaffe? Or cause him to be killed?" This privileged
debaucher was not a man likely to do his own dirty work.

Courcey had his forehead in his hands now. "No. I got
someone to ring him, when we found he'd been removed

from his church. At that Downton Hall place. To threaten him he'd better keep his mouth shut or it would be the worse for him. He'd said he felt he had to reveal what he knew about us, you see, and we couldn't have that – well, you've seen the photographs."

"And when he refused to co-operate with you, refused to agree to keep his mouth shut, you had him killed."

"No!" He looked up at them at last, his eyes at once hunted and desperate to be believed. "It's true he said he couldn't guarantee to remain silent. I don't know what would have happened, if I'm honest. I'm not the only one with a public reputation to guard, you know. But he disappeared, before we could decide what to do next. Then we heard that he was dead."

"That must have been a great relief to you."

"It was, I can tell you." In his exhaustion and despair, the words were out before he could stifle them. He looked at them dumbly, a politician shocked by his own spontaneity.

Very shortly an ex-politician, thought Peach grimly. He said, "We shall need to speak to you again in due course, in connection with our murder enquiry. And other officers will inevitably wish to interview you in a different context. You may wish to consider your position over the weekend: I think that is the correct Parliamentary phrase."

Superintendent Tucker had enjoyed his Saturday morning. He hadn't played very good golf, but he'd enjoyed the bright day and the clear air, with its early cold giving way to a sun which still had pleasing warmth in it in early September.

He didn't even mind when his companions asked about the murder of the Brunton priest over their clubhouse drinks at lunchtime. His position as the controller of the enquiry into this major local sensation made him seem rather a VIP in the bar. He gave a lordly overview of the situation and rather vague account of the progress made so far. When people pressed him for more detail, he shook his head sagely and smiled. There was much more he could tell if he chose, he implied, but they must understand that professional responsibilities forbade it at this stage. Eventually, after he had directed his team towards a few areas he had already noted as suspicious, there would be an arrest. He would reveal all to them in due course, when the time was appropriate.

All this was suggested rather than openly stated, but Tucker gave a good performance as the Great Detective. Indeed, it had become more polished with practice, for he had acted out the role in public many times. His listeners did not detect the cracks in the facade as the egregious Peach would have done. With that thought, Superintendent Tucker began wondering once again whether he could not arrange a transfer for that odious little man; let some other unfortunate have the burden of his perpetual insubordination. But that familiar vision of Eden was followed as always by its contrary note of caution. Peach, however uncomfortable he made life, got results, and it was on those results that his own reputation had largely been built. Tucker always claimed modestly that he ran the most efficient CID section in Lancashire; with retirement not too far away, he could not afford to remove the chief pillar from his temple.

These reflections over his third gin and tonic were interrupted by the club steward. There was a call for Superintendent Tucker on the members' phone in the hall. "No rest for the wicked – I was lucky to snatch the morning away!" said Thomas Tucker. He caused the maximum disturbance in the crowded lounge as he made his way between the noisy

Saturday lunchtime tables to the hall. Might as well let these people know who he was and how hard he worked.

"It's Peach, sir. Sorry to disturb you in your well-earned rest. I know it's these very necessary breaks from the routine of investigations which give you the overview we all rely on so much, and I'm naturally—"

"What is it, Peach? It had better be something bloody important, for you to disturb me here!"

"Yes, sir. Indeed, sir. Just keeping you up to date with developments in a murder case, as your guidelines say we ought to. But perhaps I'd better leave it until Monday. Use my own initiative, sort of, if you judge that this can be left to me. Yes, well, sorry to have disturbed you. I'll—"

"Oh, for God's sake, Peach what the hell is it?" The prospect of a weekend of wondering just what he had refused to hear, of worrying about what on earth Peach working on his own initiative would get up to, was worse than anything the man might produce for him now.

Peach savoured the moment, timing his bombshell to drop with maximum effect into Tommy Bloody Tucker's sanguine weekend world. "Well, I thought you'd like to know that Lucy Blake and I have been roughing up an MP this morning. Well, me, really. DS Blake didn't have a big part in it, the man not being very susceptible to a flash of suspender. Still—"

"*Peach!* You're telling me you've approached an MP without even clearing it with me first? Don't think I'm going to—"

"I was trying to tell you what I intended on Thursday, sir. After I'd talked to Joe Jackson and his scene of crime team. It was all in his report of the SOCO team's findings at the Sacred Heart presbytery. Perhaps you didn't get the chance to look at it, sir. I can't think you could possibly have overlooked it. Being as meticulous as you are, I mean, and—"

"*Peach!* I rely on you to bring me up to date and you know that. You saw me on Thursday afternoon and never mentioned—"

"Didn't get the chance, sir. 'I've plenty of things to be busy with, if you haven't. Off you go and push things forward,' you said. I took it that you were telling me to get on with things, sir, and being as the MP seemed the most urgent item, I've been to see him this morning, as soon as he was back in his constituency. While you were out on the course recharging your batteries, sir."

Game, set and match, thought Percy. You've tied yourself up neatly in the knots of your own idleness and now you can flounder in your own bullshit. He savoured both metaphors while he listened to Tucker breathing hard at the other end of the line; he could picture him thinking how he might best retrieve the shreds of his own control. It was a pleasingly lengthy pause.

Then Tucker said heavily, "I'll need to see you."

"Very well, sir. Will you come in to the station?"

Another pause, shorter this time, while Tucker worked out that an unwonted appearance at Brunton CID on a Saturday afternoon would betoken a personal panic and affect his image. "No. You'd better come round to my house."

"Right, sir. DS Blake and I are off to see another pair of suspects this afternoon – no rest for the wicked, as I believe they say. But we could call in after that. Say about half-past four? Give me the chance to meet your delightful lady wife again and—"

"You won't be meeting Barbara. This is strictly business, Peach. And come alone. The things I want to say to you aren't fit for DS Blake's ears."

"Confidential, sir? I understand. I look forward to an

103

informed exchange of information and a view from aloft on how the case stands at the moment. Good of you to make the time for me! Conscientious to a fault, as always."

Percy rang off before he could be contradicted. It was a pity when you had to work on Saturdays. But at least the Rovers were playing away. And a bit of innocent mischief always helped to lighten the day.

Nine

Keith Hanlon watched anxiously for the return of his wife. They were a close couple. When he saw her pale and distraught, as she had been for the last five weeks, it affected him too. Neither of them had slept well since they had found out about young Jamie and what had happened to him.

Pat looked bowed down with care as he saw her, shoulders slumped, coming through the gate. He knew that she was apprehensive about this interview with the CID people: he wasn't looking forward to it himself, God knew, but he'd had to pretend he was treating it lightly, to try to lift her spirits. At least they were close to each other, very close; that had carried them through other crises in their life together, and it would carry them through this. Compared with the loss of a child in infancy twelve years ago, Jamie's trouble was a minor cross to bear. The boy was in good health, and any psychological scars would soon heal, he told Pat. Boys were very resilient at that age.

But he knew that while Jamie was at the centre of this earth-shattering affair, it wasn't only their son's experience that troubled Pat. They were good church folk, the Hanlons, imbued with a serene faith when even the most devout of their contemporaries seemed shaken by doubt. They attended Sunday Mass with their four children, usually taking Communion.

105

And in an era when the sacrament of Penance had become suspect for many Catholics and a source of ridicule from those outside their Church, the Hanlons still went readily to Confession every month.

That, indeed, was part of their trouble, Keith thought. The small parish of the Sacred Heart was served by a single priest. So they had made their Confessions to Father Bickerstaffe and sought absolution from him. During the time when that man had been doing such unthinkable things with their son, the parents and children alike had been professing their sins in the darkened box of his confessional, taking the host from his fingers at Communion. It felt sometimes as if their Church as well as its minister had betrayed them. The Hanlons' whole world had collapsed.

Pat said as she came in, "Mary said it was no trouble to take them for a couple of hours – they were playing happily enough with hers when I left. She's been very good through all this, you know."

"Indeed she has. And it's good of her to take our lot on a Saturday, when she's three of her own at home. That's one of the few consolations in all this, Pat. People have been very good, very understanding."

Except for that awful woman in the supermarket, she thought, who had implied that Jamie must have led the man on, that it was really mostly his fault. She hadn't told Keith about that. He'd been so inflamed – almost unbalanced – about Father Bickerstaffe that she didn't know what he'd have done about that woman; probably gone straight round to make the woman eat her words. And that wouldn't have done anyone any good, least of all poor Jamie. She said, "It was a woman who rang to make the appointment. Detective Sergeant, she said she was. Took me by surprise, somehow, a woman being involved in things like this. Perhaps she was just making the arrangements."

As in many things, Pat Hanlon found it more comfortable to be a little behind the times. Her husband said gently, "I think women are fully involved in police work now. Even in detection, I believe."

"Still, it's not very nice for a woman, being involved in clearing up things – things like what happened to our Jamie, is it?"

She still had the image of women in the likeness of the Blessed Virgin, he thought, the source of gentleness and light, of passive suffering, like Mary at the foot of the cross. Even he knew that all women weren't like that, that modern women needed more outlets for their brains and skills – and yes, even for their goodness. He said, "It's good to have more women in the police force, I think, Pat. Women will find it more easy than us men to bring comfort into the lives of those who have been wronged, surely?"

"There should be more thought given to the victims of crime." She said it dully, as though she were repeating a political slogan, or promulgating some new Christian dogma, he thought. He wished her anger could have been more violent and spontaneous when they found out about Jamie, as his had been. She might have suffered less, in the long run. Now she looked through the window and said in the same automatic, unvarying tone, "This must be them now. A man and a woman."

Against her strange calm, Peach brought an infusion of energy into the room. "Detective Inspector Peach and Detective Sergeant Blake," he said, thrusting his hand at each of them in turn. "Good of you to see us on a Saturday afternoon. But you'll understand we want to clear this up as quickly as possible. Murder doesn't wait for anyone."

Keith found himself resenting this breezy expedition. "You can't expect us to be as keen to catch the man who killed him as you are. After what he did to our son, I mean."

"Man or woman, sir. We have an open mind on that. And I understand your feelings, but murder is murder. We can't turn any blind eyes to it."

Pat Hanlon nodded. "It's our Christian duty to give all the help we can, Keith. Father Bickerstaffe didn't deserve to be killed, whatever he did. Vengeance is the Lord's, not any man's."

"Indeed, madam. Just so." Peach, beneath his briskness, was more observant than people realised. He had already taken in that this was a family home, where the children came first and there was no doubt much love. There were toys in the corner, a series of school photographs of children at different ages, singly, but also in pairs and trios on the mantelpiece and the sideboard. The room was spotless, the twin sofas and the single armchair well worn but also well cared for. He'd put his wages on the belief that there were pictures of footballers and pop stars on the bedroom walls of the children's rooms upstairs. He walked over and picked up the picture which was in pride of place on top of the television, a family group with the parents sitting on the sofa and the four children around them. "Very nice group," he said. He pointed at the only boy. "This must be Jamie."

"That's him, yes, our eldest. He's fourteen now."

"Better tell us what happened to him, then. Best to start from the beginning, I always think."

Keith Hanlon looked for a moment as if he would refuse. Then he looked at his wife and said, "There isn't a lot to tell. But what there is is extremely distressing for us, as you may understand. Jamie joined the youth club as soon as he went to secondary school. We encouraged it, so long as it didn't affect his homework. But it seemed a good thing in that respect – he was so keen on the youth club that he got straight down to work as soon as he got home from school, worked hard at it so that he could have an hour at the youth club when he'd finished. We were glad to see him enjoying himself. And we do have three other children to look after as well, you know."

Lucy Blake said, "You shouldn't feel guilty because you didn't notice anything. Parents very rarely do. Children find it difficult to talk about anything like this, even when there's a close relationship. Sometimes that only seems to make it more difficult for them. Even when the abuse is much worse than it was in this case."

Pat Hanlon looked for a moment outraged, as if there could be no greater evil in the world than that which had befallen their boy. She said inconsequentially, "Jamie was an altar boy at the church. He served Mass for Father Bickerstaffe, quite often. There's a rota for Sundays, but Jamie served nearly every Saturday."

"And did the priest make any advance to him on those occasions?"

"No. Not after Mass." Keith Hanlon cut in quickly. "I'm sure even a man like Bickerstaffe wasn't prepared to debase the very heart of his religion with such things."

A Puritan, this, thought Percy Peach. A man not prepared to entertain the unthinkable, and thrown right off balance when it happened to him. He said, "I know you've been through this before, but tell us how you found out what was going on."

Hanlon glanced again at his wife before he began his account. "Jamie had been going to the youth club less and less frequently. It seemed odd, because he'd always enjoyed it so much and – and we knew he was quite keen on one or two of the girls who went there. In an innocent, adolescent sort of way, you understand. He's a good Catholic boy, is Jamie."

Percy recalled that expression. It was exactly what he had been, at Jamie's age. And look what had happened to him. He said hastily, "Quite. So he no longer wanted to go to the youth club. Didn't you suspect anything?"

"No. I told you, we're a busy family. He just seemed a bit moody, but that's what you expect of adolescents, isn't it?" He sounded like a man who had read it in a book, but still didn't believe his children would give him many teenage problems.

"But I understand you were the first parents to suspect what was going on. Something must have made you suspicious eventually."

Pat Hanlon said abruptly, "No, I don't think anything did. Perhaps it would have been better if we had been more suspicious by nature. We thought he was safe while he was doing things at the church, you see. We were even rather pleased about it, I think." She spoke about it wonderingly, as if it was years in the past rather than just a month ago. "Then one day he said he didn't want to serve Mass any more. I said had he got doubts about his faith and he said no, he wouldn't mind going down to serve at St Mary's in the town, but he didn't want to serve at the Sacred Heart any more. I pressed him a little about exactly why, and he suddenly collapsed into tears."

Lucy Blake felt a sharp pang of sympathy for this boy she had never met and probably never would, beset by parents at once so caring and so ignorant of the world. It was Keith Hanlon who continued the sorry tale. "I came in at that point from the office – I'm a solicitor's clerk in Brunton. I thought at first that he must have done something very wrong, when I saw his mother so upset. When I sent her away I got it out of him – got him to tell me what that – that priest had done to him." Even with the repetition of what he had now told several times his breath became uneven with emotion. It could not have been easy for the boy with this clumsy innocent of a parent, thought Lucy. He must have had to be very explicit before his father accepted what had been going on.

She said, "Forgive me, but we need the detail, and I'm sure none of us wants to take Jamie through this again. What exactly did Bickerstaffe do to Jamie?"

The Hanlons didn't ask why they wanted this, didn't realise that it was because they were interested in the parents' reactions to what had happened, not the thing itself. They were so innocent, so used to unthinking obedience to authority, that they perhaps scarcely realised in their emotional state that they were being studied as murder suspects. Unexpectedly, it was Pat Hanlon, speaking as though the details held an awful fascination, who said, "Father Bickerstaffe touched him, wanted to stroke his legs. Then he put his hand down Jamie's trousers and – and fondled him. Then the priest took him into a private room at the back of the hall and – well, he tried to get Jamie to touch his . . . his thing." She shuddered, looked for a moment as if she might be physically sick and then went on. "Apparently he said it was just a bit of fun, that it was part of growing up for boys like Jamie, that he'd enjoy it once he got used to it. It went on all the time, Father said, and Jamie should try it if he wanted to get extra pleasure out of life."

She had stared unseeingly through the window as she took them through all of this. Now she turned and looked at them, as if surprised to see them giving her such attention, and said, "That's all, I think."

Peach said, "It didn't go any further than that? There wasn't any force used, any suggestion of rape?"

Keith Hanlon looked as if it was the first time he had even considered the idea that things might actually have been a lot worse. "No. When Jamie resisted, he didn't use any physical force, I suppose. But you must understand that our boy had no idea what was going on."

Unless Jamie had picked up a little smutty schoolboy suggestion from school, thought Percy, he wouldn't be forearmed in this innocent home, least of all against a priest. He would have had the ritual 'don't talk to strange men', but in this house 'men' would never include priests. He said, "And what were your reactions when you found out what had been happening, Mr Hanlon?"

An exchange of glances between man and wife; a tiny nod of encouragement from Pat before Keith Hanlon answered. In that moment, Peach and Blake knew that they had rehearsed this together, had worked out that he would answer and what he would say. Well, there was nothing surprising in that: they must have expected this question from the moment that they heard that Bickerstaffe's body had been found. Hanlon's words had the ring of a prepared statement as he said, "It threw us right off balance, as you would expect. We knew these things went on in the world, but the last person we'd have expected them from was a priest."

So all the current debate about celibacy, all the discussions of the psychological impacts of a solitary life for people who were not living in an enclosed community, had passed this couple by. There were none so blind as those pious innocents who did not wish to see, thought Percy, indulging for a moment his own prejudices. He said, "I expect you went up to the Sacred Heart presbytery to have it out with Father Bickerstaffe."

"No. I wanted to, but Pat persuaded me that it wouldn't be wise." He looked at his wife again to gather the confidence to continue. And with that look, Peach believed that there had indeed been no confrontation between the two men, for he realised suddenly that it had been a relief for this man not to go to see the offending priest, that he would not have known how to confront the agent of the unthinkable.

"You did nothing?"

"Oh yes, we did something. We went through the proper channels." There was a ring of irony in the way he said the phrase, from this least ironic of men. Perhaps he regretted now that he had not raced off to confront the man who had abused his son, that he had let the boy down in a situation that called for emotion, not reason. "I rang Canon O'Leary at St Mary's. He gave me the name of a man in the diocese whose job it was to deal with such things." He looked as if he was surprised even after his eyes had been opened that there should be such a man available.

"And he saw you quickly?"

"Very quickly. He came over from Manchester the same night. I rang at seven-thirty and he was with us within two hours."

I'll bet he was, thought Peach grimly – rushing to put the lid on this before it got to the ears of the police. Lucky for him he was dealing with so dutiful a Catholic as Keith Hanlon. But perhaps not so lucky for Bickerstaffe, in the long run. He said sardonically, "I expect he asked you not to contact the police."

Hanlon caught his tone, rushed even in this to defend his Church and its servants. "No. He said that was our right, if we chose to use it. That we could still choose to use that right, even if what he proposed didn't work to our satisfaction. But our first thoughts must be for Jamie and the impact this would have on him. He said he had experience of court cases where children had to give evidence. In his experience, it had usually been traumatic for them. He said he would go and talk to Father Bickerstaffe, see what he had to say for himself. Then he'd come back to us and discuss what should be done next."

Percy was compelled to a reluctant admiration for this unseen negotiator. He seemed a clever bugger, which was almost the highest accolade accorded in the Peach catalogue. He said neutrally, "So you agreed that that was what he should do?"

"Yes. You must remember that at this time we thought Jamie was the only boy involved." Bet this clever bugger who came to see them didn't, thought Peach. Bet he knew the pattern, knew what to expect underneath when he turned over the stone. Hanlon went on, "Mr Farrell was as good as his word. He rang the presbytery from our house, went up to see Father Bickerstaffe that night, although it was after half-past ten. I don't know how long he was up there, but he came back to see us the next day, as promised. We found then that there were other boys involved, that Jamie wasn't the only one, apparently not even the first."

"And he persuaded you that you should not go to the police."

"Yes. He said he was a kind of trouble-shooter, that he had experience of these things. The less publicity involved, the better for the children, he said."

And the better for Holy Mother Church, thought Peach sourly. Sweep it under the carpet; behave as though it hadn't happened, as though priests were not subject to the temptations and the failures of other men, as though this was a one-off case. "And obviously you went along with that advice, or we shouldn't now be hearing about it for the first time. I'm still trying to get a clear picture of this. I'm sure my own reaction would have been to race off and thump the man who had done this to my son. Would you please tell me again, Mr Hanlon, what your feelings were about Father Bickerstaffe when you found out that this had happened?"

A quick glance again at his wife before he replied, as if he needed the reassurance of her support before he spoke. "I told you: I was devastated. At first I couldn't believe it. Then, when I had to, things moved so quickly. All within the same evening we had heard the news, we were visited by people who seemed to know all about these things and we had agreed to go along with the solution they suggested. There – well, there didn't seem to be time to digest anything, somehow. I remember us both sitting in this room at one o'clock in the morning, not saying much to each other, still not quite able to believe what had happened."

"And what about the following morning, and the days which followed that?"

Suddenly, without anyone turning to her, Pat Hanlon took up the dialogue. "Keith was angry, very angry, as anyone would be. I was as furious as he was, but in a different way, almost as if I had myself been defiled by what that man had done to Jamie. Keith wanted to go up to the Sacred Heart and have it out with him, but I knew that he wasn't rational, that he might actually strike the man who had disgraced his cloth and defiled our son." Even now, Peach thought, the magic of the priesthood held strong in this pious household, so that it was not clear which of these two things had shocked her more.

"So you persuaded him not to confront Father Bickerstaffe."

"Yes. We've all worshipped at St Mary's since then. We shall go back to the Sacred Heart now that we know that it will be served by a different priest."

Now that it is cleared of that malign influence, thought

115

Peach. Or now that you have eliminated this man who has done the unthinkable from God's earth? He said tersely, "I must address this question to both of you. Had you anything to do with the death of John Bickerstaffe?"

This time they did not look at each other. They stared straight ahead and said, "No," almost in unison. Hanlon added an "Of course not" which sounded peculiarly lame in this dramatic context.

"You will have gathered that we are treating his death as murder. Have you any idea, then, who might have killed him?"

On this, they did accord each other that now-familiar look of mutual support. Then Keith Hanlon said, "No. We were as shocked as anyone when we heard the news. We know that others have suffered as we have done, but I can't think that anyone would do this."

To a priest, he had almost said, thought Percy. He was suddenly sick of this suffocatingly pious atmosphere, wondering what it obfuscated, how much it was being used to mask the naked human passions of hatred and revenge. He said harshly, "We need a full account of your movements on Thursday the twentieth of August. Both of you."

This time Pat Hanlon gave her husband a little smile as they looked at each other, as if to say, 'Don't worry! We anticipated this. And it means the ordeal is almost over'. But even if that is indeed what she intended, thought Lucy Blake as she prepared to write down the details, it could all be perfectly innocent: the guiltless as well as the guilty felt the tension of involvement in a murder investigation.

Keith Hanlon didn't make the pretence of being uncertain, of not having anticipated this question. He said, "I was in the office for most of the day. At about three thirty, I took some documents over to Preston, to Arkright and Sons, Solicitors, in Fishergate. You can easily check it with them, but I must have arrived there soon after four, stayed for about ten minutes, and then left. My boss in Brunton had said it wasn't worth going back into the office that afternoon, so I did a little shopping in Preston and then came back home. I suppose it must have been five to five-thirty when I got back here."

There was scarcely a pause before Pat Hanlon said, "You can't check on me quite as easily as Keith. I work three mornings a week in a pre-school nursery. Thursday isn't one of them. So, as far as I can remember, I was in the house or the garden here almost all day on that Thursday. I think I went down to the bakery near here for some bread early in the afternoon, and then I was here until Keith came in as he said – I can't be any more precise than he is about the exact time that was, but it was certainly some time after five."

They looked at each other for confirmation, with the air of inexperienced amateur actors, relieved to have delivered their lines without a prompt. Lucy Blake, hoping she would be able to decipher her improvised shorthand later, said, "Is there anyone who can verify these late afternoon times?"

Pat Hanlon shrugged. "Only the children. And I'd rather they weren't brought into this, if it can be avoided. The whole thing has been quite disturbing enough for them."

"It shouldn't be necessary for us to speak to them," said Peach. He frowned from one to the other of the parents, his black eyebrows beetling beneath the shining dome of his baldness. "Not at this stage, anyway. What about the rest of that evening?"

Keith Hanlon was straight in on the heels of the question, as if he had been waiting for his cue. "We were here. Did half an hour in the garden, tidying up the borders, then

117

watched television for the rest of the night, as far as I can remember."

You can remember, thought Peach grimly. You could give me the programmes, probably describe their content, if you were pressed. But what did all that mean? This pair were so versed in piety, so controlled by religious behaviour for years, that it provided a natural shield for them against outsiders, one of which they were probably not even aware.

He said, "If either of you thinks of anything which might help us to arrest a murderer, it's your duty to let us know immediately." He was at the door before Lucy Blake had closed her notebook and stood up. He had only just avoided saying 'your Christian duty'.

In the front garden of Superintendent Thomas Tucker, the roses bloomed in their September glory. Roses were a cliché of well-being in the police world. An established bed of them betokened that their cultivator had enjoyed a certain degree of success, felt that he would not have to move house again, and was looking towards his pension and a serene retirement. And Tommy Bloody Tucker's roses certainly wouldn't be short of bullshit, Percy Peach reflected, as he walked between them to the front door of the solid Edwardian house.

The door opened as if by some electric signal as he approached. Tucker's head appeared beside it like that of an apprehensive tortoise surveying the world beyond its shell. "Come into the front room," he said, and led his Inspector stealthily across the high hall.

"He hasn't told that harridan of a wife I was coming. He's frightened to death of a bollocking for bringing his work home at the weekend," Percy Peach divined happily. Percy had nicknamed Mrs Tucker the great auk. Most people thought it was simply a reference to her large and prominent Roman nose, but Percy would point out to whoever would listen that the formidable Barbara was obviously 'fowl' and should certainly be extinct. She must be perched in the rear regions of this large house, or Tucker would not have been so furtive.

"What's all this about visiting our MP without my permission?" the Superintendent began when he had shut the door. He found it difficult to be angry in a low voice.

"Been buggering about with children, sir. I thought it my duty," said Peach stiffly, standing to attention like a young constable. Then he added, "And almost literally, we believe, sir!" He smiled with a sudden contentment that his language should be so accurate.

"Now look, Peach, if you're going to convince me that Mrs Bradbury has been assaulting children, you'll need to be very sure indeed of your ground. If I'm—"

"Oh no, sir! Ha, ha, ha!" Peach's theatrical laugh set the chandelier tinkling and made Tucker look fearfully towards the rear of the house. "Not Elsie Bradbury. The very idea! Ha, ha! You mustn't go spreading rumours about our Elsie round the town." Elsie Bradbury had been the Labour MP for Brunton for thirty years, holding her seat narrowly through the dark days of Thatcherism and triumphantly with the revival of the party under the man she called affectionately 'Our young Turk, Mr Blair.' She was a model MP, in her seventies and respected by all parties in the house. The town's large health centre and other amenities stemmed from her tireless championing of the area. "You mustn't attack our Elsie, sir, however much you feel tempted. Unless you have genuine grounds for suspicion, of course. If you'd like me to make a few inquiries into her background, in my own discreet way, then I'll—"

119

"Peach, shut up and tell me who the hell this MP was!"

Tucker's voice had the intensity of a man near to his breaking point, and Percy took heed. "Charles Courcey, sir. MP for the Hodder Valley. Oh, he tried to come the 'de Courcey' with me, but I wasn't having that. I reminded him about his father's bankruptcy and—"

"Peach! You haven't been annoying Charles Courcey?"

"Yes, sir. I have, sir!" Peach, who still hadn't been asked to sit down, moved to the sheepskin rug in front of the green-tiled fireplace and beamed, like a schoolboy awaiting the approval of a fond parent.

Tucker's jaw had dropped, and for a moment it looked as if it would stay dropped. Then he said in anguished woe, "But Charles Courcey is a Grand Master!"

"Yes, sir. Master of trouser-dropping, if you ask me. Master of rent-boys, perhaps. Master of—"

"Grand Master of his Lodge, I mean, you fool! Courcey is a very important man, Peach, who can do you and me a lot of damage."

"Ah, the Masons, sir." The puzzlement lifted in slow motion from Percy's face and was replaced by a beatific smile, as he simulated comprehension of this news. "But that doesn't leave him free from prosecution, sir, does it? Not unless I've missed some circular from the Crown Prosecution Service, which is always possible, of course, the rate they fire bumf out these days. The computer and the photocopier have a lot to answer for, if you ask me, and it's not impossible that—"

"*Peach!*" Tucker's shout stemmed the torrent of words from his abominable visitor, but he was immediately aware that it must have penetrated the nethermost regions of the house. He lowered his voice again. "Of course Masons have no special privileges when it comes to the law. I'm just saying you have to be careful, that's all. My God, man, you've no grasp at all of public relations."

Percy shook his head sadly. "No, sir, I'm sure you're right. It's just that I thought paedophiles weren't good news, and paedophile rings should be tackled as soon as possible. I seem to remember a memo from you on those lines a few months ago. If there's been a change of policy, I missed it."

He had lost patience with the game now, and the two men stood eyeing each other for a moment in open hostility. Then Tucker said, "If he's a paedophile, of course he must be pursued. I'm only saying that we must proceed with a little caution and—"

"Courcey's a paedophile, sir. And a member of a ring exchanging child pornography. And involved in a murder case. I didn't think it was a moment for too much caution."

Tucker stared at his DI in horror. His own modest ambition to be Master of his Lodge seemed to him to be washed away on this flood of bad news. "Courcey is involved in the Bickerstaffe murder?"

"Involved, sir, certainly. Not necessarily guilty of pulling the cord round the poor bugger's neck himself. Perhaps not involved at all in the murder: that remains to be seen. But he's already tried to suppress evidence."

Tucker sat down, suddenly and heavily, on the brass-studded leather armchair by the fireplace. "You'd better tell me all about it," he said dully.

Peach did. When he had enlarged upon his views of the Courcey paedophilia ring, he also brought his chief up to date on the news from Downton Hall, and reported on the interviews with Kate Maxted and the Hanlons. He remained standing with feet astride on the sheepskin rug throughout. Then he took his leave of Tommy Bloody Tucker.

As the man led him covertly back across the hall, Percy called cheerfully towards the distant door to the kitchen, "Goodbye, Mrs Tucker. Sorry I didn't have time to renew our acquaintance."

Ten

There is a connection between intensity and psychological disturbance. There are too many exceptions for the association to be very useful, and psychiatrists find intensity far too wide and all-embracing a term for it to be valuable. Percy Peach affected a fine contempt for both psychologists and psychiatrists, but he had met a few very intense psychopaths in his time, one of whom had made a violent attempt to emasculate him with a meat hook.

He therefore noted with a wary interest that one of the men whose sons had been assaulted by the late Father John Bickerstaffe seemed very intense indeed. David Kennedy was older than any other of the parents involved in this affair. He was fifty-seven, a research chemist who worked in the laboratories of the electrical company which was a major employer in Brunton since the decline of the cotton industry.

Although he had agreed the time of this interview on the phone with Lucy Blake, he opened the door no more than three inches and peered at the police duo with dark suspicion. He inspected their warrants, gave no answering smile to DS Blake's assurance that they had spoken on the phone earlier that morning, and treated them like a determined atheist beset by Jehovah's Witnesses. He was a man with crinkly grey hair, a lined, worried face and years more appropriate to a grandparent than a parent. Eventually he said reluctantly, "I suppose you'd better come in."

They went into a square room which was almost obsessively neat. No sign here of the toys they had noted in the Hanlons' house; there was a modern desk under the window, a small cottage-style three piece suite, prints of what looked like Chester on the walls. A compact hi-fi tower stood in one corner of the room, but there was no television set. As if he registered their thoughts, Kennedy said, "The boys don't come in here much. They prefer the back room with the television. I like to keep this place tidy."

Lucy Blake said, "You have two sons, I believe."

"Yes. Liam is sixteen now. It was Thomas, my younger son, who had the trouble at the youth club." He spoke without hesitation or embarrassment. Obviously it was the euphemism he had decided upon and he would stick to that phrase.

"And you live here alone with your sons?"

"Yes. My wife and I were divorced six years ago. I was given custody of the children." He had addressed all his remarks to her, as if he found it easier to talk to her than to Peach. Yet he had a monkish look; one might have anticipated that this ageing ascetic would have been soured towards all women by the failure of his marriage.

Because he seemed almost to expect it, Lucy said, "It's unusual for a man to be given custody when a marriage breaks down, isn't it?"

"She went off with someone much younger than me. She didn't want the boys. They'd have got in the way of her new lifestyle." He looked past her, not at her, while he spoke the bare phrases. He had a slight, mirthless smile and she wondered how much anguish his staccato delivery of the facts concealed. Yet it was he who had led her to those facts, he who had seemed to want the family background made clear.

In an attempt to bring his attention back to her, she said, "The authorities must have felt you would provide a good home for the lads, or they wouldn't have left them with you."

He smiled at her then, the first real warmth they had felt from him. "We get on well enough together, the three of us. We're all odd in our own ways, but most of humanity is like that. The problems come when people don't recognise it."

This sounded dangerously like philosophy to Percy Peach. Philosophy wasn't as bad as sociology or psychology, but it was suspect, and he took it as a cue to intervene. "Difficult for the boys, though, not having a mother."

"Not as difficult for them as having a bad mother. An increasing number of children have to manage without one parent or another, these days, Inspector. Or has that escaped your notice?"

Sarcasm was a brave weapon to employ against Peach. He looked at Kennedy with his head on one side for a moment, his face expressionless save for a widening of the dark eyes beneath his bald dome. With his black moustache, he looked for all the world like a miniature Oliver Hardy, about to hit poor Stan Laurel over the head for his latest *faux pas*. Then he said, "It hasn't escaped my notice, no. Many of those children end up in the hands of the police, you see. Their lawyers usually offer a bad home environment as mitigating circumstances when their offences come to court. But I'm glad to hear you're coping manfully. Came to grief up at the youth club though, didn't he, your Thomas?"

For a moment, Lucy thought Kennedy was going to spring at Peach. Then he controlled himself, forced himself to fold his arms as he sat in his armchair opposite his tormentor. The effort it cost him was evident in the unevenness of his breathing as he said, "That would have happened if Thomas had had both parents and his grandparents around. That man – that so-called priest – deceived other people as well as us."

He was unable to bring himself to name Bickerstaffe, just as he had been unable to bring himself to name his wife, thought Peach. Ascetic men were often unable to name the thing they found most loathsome, just as frigid women could not name the organs of sex. He said, "That seems to be true enough. You had no suspicions about what was going on up there?"

"No. The parents are often the last to know in these cases, it seems. Liam had attended the youth club for a year or so, with no trouble. When Thomas seemed to be enjoying himself up there, I thought it a good thing for him to be mixing like that."

He was defending himself now, a thing he had never expected or intended to do, thought Lucy. Percy's penchant for getting under people's skins usually made them reveal more about themselves than a more polite approach. Peach said, "Probably it was a good thing for young Thomas, until this happened. Brought him into contact with the opposite sex, for one thing. Excellent thing that, when he was living in an all-male household."

"He's barely fourteen. And there are girls enough in his class at school."

"Not the same, though, is it? Bit of social mixing, outside school hours, not under the eagle eye of teachers or parents, good thing, I should think. Not that I've any kids myself. Must be difficult, handling adolescents on your own."

Kennedy looked at him, calmer now, but not troubling to conceal his dislike. "We get by. We have our ups and downs, but we get by. Is this leading anywhere?"

"Not sure, really. It's giving us a picture, I suppose. Roman Catholic yourself, are you, Mr Kennedy?"

"No. I don't have much time for any established religion. My wife was a Catholic, and I allowed the boys to be christened in that church, on condition they were allowed to make their own minds up about religion as they got older. I may say they have now rejected it." He could not restrain a look of satisfaction.

Peach himself had been brought up in an atmosphere of stifling, unquestioning piety, of priests in elaborate robes and thuribles swinging with incense. In due course, when he was about nineteen, he had rejected it all. Somehow he felt the boys in this house, wrestling with the problems of belief when they were no more than children, under pressure from a father longing to hear them declare their agnosticism, had had things much worse than he had. He said, "But you didn't object to the lads attending a Catholic youth club."

Kennedy spread out his hands without moving his arms: it was a curiously cramped gesture with which to indicate his liberality. "I am a broad-minded man, Inspector Peach," he said, apparently unaware that his appearance and bearing had indicated exactly the opposite to them. "If they enjoy themselves in an environment where the religious overtones can only be minimal, I have no objection. And one of today's religious buzz-words is 'ecumenical', so the club officially welcomes all faiths. I don't think there are many kids there without Roman Catholic connections, mind you."

"There won't be now, at any rate," said Peach robustly. "Not when the news of Father Shirtlifter gets round the town. And it will, you know, however much they try to hush it up. The victim's background is bound to come out during the murder trial, for one thing."

"You think his death is connected with his offences?"

"Oh, I'd expect so, wouldn't you? There are plenty of people still around who think hanging's the appropriate penalty for child abuse. It was probably one of them. Bickerstaffe was garrotted with a piece of thin rope or wire. About as near as you could get to hanging." Percy, that bitter opponent of psychology, beamed happily at this awful amateur sally into its realms.

There was a sound of movement behind the door at the rear of the room. David Kennedy called, "Thomas? Come in here, will you?"

A thin boy, who looked less than his fourteen years, came reluctantly through the doorway, blushing furiously behind his horn-rimmed spectacles. Peach wondered if he had been listening behind the door, and the boy's first words confirmed his suspicions. "I just came in from the back," he said. "My bike's got a puncture and I'm trying to repair it."

"This is Detective Sergeant Blake and this is Detective Inspector Peach," said his father, and the boy shook hands solemnly with each of them in turn. "They're just here to ask a few questions. I knew they were coming."

The boy nodded abstractedly, as if he did not need such reassurance. "Are you here to find out who killed Father Bickerstaffe?" he said.

Lucy smiled at him, but received no answering grin. He stood there a little owlishly, head on one side, full of a gauche intelligence. She hoped there was no bullying at his school, for he looked a classic victim for the unthinking cruelties of teenage boys. "We don't expect to find that out by speaking to your father, Thomas. But we are trying to find out facts about Father Bickerstaffe, yes. And eventually, when we assemble enough facts, we shall know who killed him."

"I hope you find who did it. He wasn't a bad man, you

know. He just liked – well, touching people. He went a bit too far, that's all. But he stopped, when he knew you really wanted him to. It was partly my own fault, you see. I should have stopped him earlier than I did."

David Kennedy, who had watched him indulgently until now, said with sudden harshness, "There is no blame attached to you, Thomas. None at all. We've had all this out before. I think you'd better get back to your bike now, leave us to sort this out; I don't suppose we'll be long."

They looked more like grandfather and grandson than father and son, and the boy ignored him, did not even look at him. He repeated, his old-young face taut with the thought, "I hope you find who killed him. He was a good man, really. He didn't deserve to be killed like that."

They divined in that moment that he thought his father might have done this, that this puny figure was wracked at nights by the thought that the only adult who was close to him might have done this awful, unthinkable thing. He needed to talk, perhaps for hours, to someone who would listen with more understanding and sympathy than this anchorite of a father. Peach smiled at him, said with more kindness than Lucy had seen in him before, "You're right, Thomas. We're trying to build up a picture of Father Bickerstaffe – that's the way we work, you see, when someone's been killed like this. And it's good to hear from you that you thought he had these good qualities. We'll find out who killed him in due course, don't you worry about that."

The boy looked with them at his father to see his reaction. David Kennedy managed a strained smile. He said, "Your generosity does you credit, Tom. I don't think you can help us here, though." It was the first time he had used the diminutive of the boy's name, and it emerged as an appeal. His son looked at him for a moment, nodded abruptly, and turned to leave the room. But the politeness which had been bred into him was too strong for him to leave like that: at the door he remembered his manners, turned and said, "I'll say goodbye, then."

"Goodbye, Thomas," said the detectives in unison and the boy, reduced again to the embarrassed young teenager who had come so diffidently into the room, slipped out of it again. He had lost his self-consciousness only in the moments when he had spoken of the dead man and the search for his killer.

It was the first time they had seen any of the children who had been abused by Bickerstaffe. Both of them had been called upon to investigate much greater abuses of children than those perpetrated by that sad and lonely figure John Bickerstaffe. But the sight of that slight, bespectacled boy, still not quite certain of how seriously he had been affected by what had happened, reminded them vividly of the traumas of abuse, of the passions which must have been aroused in the very different homes affected by the dead priest's activities.

Peach did not moderate the aggression of his approach to Kennedy with that thought. "Difficult for you, when you found out what had been going on up at that youth club. Being a single-parent family, I mean. And an all-male one, at that. And you so much older than most fathers, with such an age gap to breach to get close to your children."

Kennedy seemed about to flare up at that. Then he said through clenched teeth, "We coped. We've coped with worse than that, in our time."

"Really? Tell me how you coped, Mr Kennedy. When did you hear?"

"About the middle of August. A man called Farrell came round and asked to speak to me. He said he had the authority of the diocese. He was employed to counsel people, when things like this happened, he said. It became obvious as we talked that he was a kind of trouble-shooter for situations like this. It shows how many of them they have." The last phrase came out with triumphant satisfaction, as if even amidst this personal tragedy he could not resist noting this corruption in a religion he despised.

"And you knew nothing of what had been going on before this?"

"No. Thomas hadn't said anything to me. Apparently Liam suspected, from one or two things he'd let drop. And Thomas had decided he wasn't going to go up there any more. But I didn't have any inkling of the abuse until that man Farrell arranged to see me. There were others as well as Thomas, he told me."

"There were indeed. We are speaking to all the parents involved. What was your reaction when you heard, Mr Kennedy?"

"I was shocked, of course. But not really too surprised, when I thought about it. Celibacy is an unnatural state for a man. Any religion which favours it is asking for trouble like that." Again the personal tragedy was translated into a general attack upon an institution. They were left wondering how celibate a life Kennedy himself had led since the departure of his wife. He had the intensity of a man whose personality was off-balance. A man who would surely need a more personal outlet for his reaction to his son's suffering than a particular religion.

"Did you go to see Father Bickerstaffe?"

"I tried to. This chap Farrell who came round didn't want me to, but after we'd talked to Thomas and found just what Bickerstaffe had done, I felt I wanted to confront the man. I rang the presbytery and made an appointment to see him the next night, but when I went up there, he wasn't there and his housekeeper either didn't know or wouldn't tell me where he'd gone."

"And what would you have done, if you had been able to confront him?"

"I don't know. Had it out with him."

"And what would that have involved?"

"I don't know. How can I, when it never happened?"

"It's a legitimate question, nonetheless. You must see that, now that the man lies dead in the mortuary and we are investigating his murder."

"Perhaps. But I have no very clear idea of what I would have done."

"Would you have offered him violence? Did you plan to hit him?"

"No . . . I don't know. It would have depended on what attitude he took, I suppose." Suddenly, this very still figure ran both hands through his grey hair, a gesture more startling because he had been so static before it.

"Did you speak to your ex-wife about what had happened?"

"Yes. I thought it was perhaps my duty to let her know, even though the boys didn't want me to."

"And how did she react?"

"Hysterically. She screamed about the priest, even though she hadn't seen the boys for over a year. Talked about vengeance." He shook his head sadly, but they could see he took some satisfaction from the uncontrolled and unhelpful reaction of this mother he now despised. "The boys were right – I shouldn't have bothered to inform her."

"Tell us where you were on the afternoon and evening of August twentieth, please."

The grey eyes flashed a look of open hostility at his

interlocutor. "That's when he died, isn't it? You think I might have killed him."

"Yes. I think any one of half a dozen people might have killed him. It's my job to think like that, you see. And to ask the right questions."

Even Lucy Blake was shocked by Peach's directness, by his refusal to back off into the comfortable platitudes they all used at times. Perhaps he had sensed the contempt in which his occupation was held by the ascetic individual on the other side of the room; perhaps, as usual, he was playing this rally by instinct, that instinct which so often sought out the weakness in other people's temperaments.

Kennedy was clearly upset by his bluntness, but could find no flaw in his logic. He said, "I can't remember where I was, at this distance."

"Were you at your place of work on that afternoon?"

"I expect so. And before you ask, I don't clock on and clock off, so there won't be any convenient record for you."

"Or for you, Mr Kennedy. It would be convenient for both of us if you could be eliminated from this enquiry."

"I was probably late home. I often am on a Thursday. We have a meeting where we assess what we have been doing and plan the following week's work."

"So what time would you have arrived here on that night?"

"About seven thirty, I suppose. I leave a frozen cottage pie or something like that, and Liam heats it up for the two of them in the microwave. The boys could confirm that."

But what they couldn't confirm is where you were between five and half-past seven, thought Peach. And you know that as well as I do, David Kennedy.

*   *   *

Percy Peach got his game of golf on Sunday afternoon. What is more, he played where town met country, in the clear bright air of the North Lancashire Golf Club, not the more plebeian Brunton Golf Club, where Superintendent Tucker was forced to hack his way round. Tucker had been rejected by the North Lancs because he could not meet the handicap requirements; it was a rebuttal which had been made the more bitter a year or so ago, when the North Lancs had accepted the younger and more proficient Inspector Peach with alacrity.

Percy, who had been a batsman skilful enough to take on the professionals in the Lancashire League, had initially found golf a frustrating game. But today, when he was content just to be away from the job for a few hours and breathe deep of the moorland air, he played well. The match was over by the fifteenth, but Percy finished with a flourish by making a birdie at the difficult eighteenth. He and his partner pocketed their modest winnings, showered, and sat exchanging banter over pints of bitter in the thinly peopled bar. As in all civilised places, personal phones were banned in the clubhouse, so Percy retired to the privacy of a cubicle in the gents' cloakroom to ring in to the station to check if there were any messages for him.

It was in that unlikely spot that the investigation into the murder of the Reverend John Bickerstaffe took an unexpected turn. "There's been one call for you, Percy. A woman called Cartwright. Apparently you and Lucy Blake had arranged to see the Cartwrights tomorrow afternoon."

"Yes. They're the last of the parents whose sons were touched up by John the Lad. Cartwright's self-employed, so he's able to get away to see us then."

"That's right. But this call was from Mrs Cartwright. She

134

wants you to go in the morning, when her husband isn't there. She says there are things you ought to know about what Bickerstaffe did to her son. And she wants the boy to be there himself."

Eleven

Superintendent Tucker was determined to assert himself.
"Now look here, Peach! Just sit down and listen, will
you?" DS Peach dropped gracefully on to the seat before the
big desk, as attentive and alert as a vigilant panther. "Just don't
speak until I've finished what I have to say. I don't want your
silly comments making me lose my thread. Now, this MP.
You've gone charging in without my permission, trampling
all over any sense of decorum, ignoring the protocol which
any reasonable officer knows must be observed in dealing with
VIPs. You have embarrassed me personally, and what is more I
am sure it will emerge in due course that you have embarrassed
the Brunton force as a whole. I've been thinking about this over
the weekend, and what emerges is that you've gone too far this
time. Well, have you *nothing* to say for yourself?"

Peach's eyes widened alarmingly. His almost non-existent
neck disappeared completely as his shoulders rose towards
his ears. He gave every appearance of a man seized by a
paroxysm. Finally his control broke and breath burst out like
a missile from his overtaxed lungs. "Beg pardon sir! You said
I wasn't to speak. Wasn't to offer any of my silly comments.
Has that order now been rescinded?"

Tucker sighed, resisting the impulse to hurl the paperweight
on his desk at the earnest bald dome which he surely could not

have missed. "You're not a boy soldier on an army parade, Peach – however infantile your behaviour may be. I expect some form of reaction when I give you a dressing-down."

"Yes, sir. Some form of reaction: I'll try to remember. Thank you, sir."

"Now, what you've got to do is to try to retrieve the situation. An apology is called for. If Charles Courcey is still in the constituency, you must arrange to see him personally and tell him that you were over-reacting, that it was merely an excess of zeal which led you to make the accusations you did. Oh, I don't say you shouldn't investigate him, but there are ways and means, Peach. Ways and means. MPs are influential men, controlling the destiny of all of us, and that is a fact that you should bear in mind when you go blundering into situations which you can't handle."

He doesn't know, thought Percy. Oh, thank you, God, he doesn't know! He hasn't heard the radio or television news this morning, he hasn't seen the papers. "Yes, sir. I'll do whatever you say, of course. You have an overview which those of us beavering away at the crimeface don't always perceive. Even now, when most of the public might not think we should be going easy on a wanker like Courcey, you see things which the rest of us are missing, put the whole of CID out on a limb because you see a reward which none of the rest of us can even envisage at this moment. I must say it's wonderful to have the responsibility for a controversial course of action accepted by a Superintendent who can see just what the issues—"

"Controversial?" Tucker seized on the danger-word in this seething linguistic torrent. "What do you mean, controversial?"

Percy noted the rising note of panic with the approval of a connoisseur. "Well, I just thought with him resigning and going into hiding, you wouldn't want to be associated with him. Still, if he's a friend of yours, you'd want to stick by him, I know, however courageous a course that might seem to others without your integrity."

The danger-words were tumbling one upon another now. 'Controversial' had been followed by 'courageous' and 'integrity'. Tucker felt the sweat breaking out, hot then swiftly cold, under his armpits, round his crotch, at his temples. He repeated hoarsely, "Resigning? In hiding?"

"You haven't heard the news, sir? Too busy worrying about the various cares of office, I expect. Too busy safeguarding the people who depend—"

"I had to take the dog for his walk. Barbara went to the over-fifties keep fit. The little devil ran away from me."

Peach was torn between the twin visions of the large and lumpen Barbara Tucker in a leotard and of her husband chasing a disobedient Yorkshire terrier. He stared blissfully over his chief's head and said, "You didn't have time to listen to the news, then?"

"I didn't even have time for bloody breakfast, Peach. What the hell has been going on?"

"Charles Courcey handed his resignation to the leader of the Conservative Party last night, sir. Personal reasons, he said. There's a witch-hunt on, but the Press haven't been able to find him. Rumour is, he's skipped off abroad. Paedophilia squad want to interview him – that's got out to the papers. Discreet leak from party headquarters, I should think." Peach's round face lit up with a sudden thought. "I say, sir, you aren't hiding him at your place, are you? I remember you saying on Saturday that he was a Grand Master. Very brave it would be, but I know you wouldn't let an old friend down, and I suppose in Masonic circles—"

"Courcey is no friend of mine, Peach. Never will be, never

has been. Get that into your thick skull. I want you to register it and remember it. Is that quite clear?"

Percy allowed a look of puzzlement to creep back over his features by degrees. It was a considerable performance, extending over several long seconds. "But I thought you said just now that I was to apologise to him? It's going to be difficult with him not around, and it won't be popular with the paedophilia squad or the public, but I'm sure I can do something. Perhaps if I put a statement out to the Press on your behalf, saying that he's a good chap and we're sorry if we ruffled his feathers, it would—"

"Peach! Will you for God's sake shut up and let me think? Of course, today's news puts a new slant on things, a new slant altogether."

"No need to apologise, sir?"

"No. Of course not. In fact, you should be out there trying to find out if he has any connection at all with the murder of Bickerstaffe, not wasting my time here with your inanities."

"Yes, sir. Right away, sir. I'll get back on to the case this instant. And if Courcey or any other of your Masonic friends have been chasing little boys' bums or murdering priests, I'll make sure you're the first to know."

What a lovely way to begin the week, thought Percy. What a way to cheer up a Monday morning! His heart sang with the joy of it as he went back down the stairs to rejoin the real world.

He picked up DS Blake and went to see Mrs Cartwright without her husband, as the lady had requested.

Joan Cartwright was not at all what they had expected. She was a blonde, blue-eyed woman in her early forties, running a little to fat if you were a cruel woman, pleasantly plump if you were a lascivious male. She had her hair cut to a medium length, but its severity was removed by the wide waves which curved it gracefully to her neck; her regular, rounded features were set into a face which seemed to drop into a smile as its normal expression. DS Lucy Blake thought she was a pleasant, maternal woman, who seemed anxious to help. DI Percy Peach, who had gathered some experience in the field after his marriage ended, thought she was every lonely drinker's ideal of a friendly barmaid.

The one way in which she conformed to their expectations was that she was apprehensive. She greeted them at the door of the modern detached house, glanced like a nervous tortoise from side to side as they introduced themselves, and led them swiftly into a lounge dominated by a huge three-piece suite, as comfortable and rounded in its contours as the lady of the house. Peach sank into an armchair which threatened to envelop him and said, "We came to see you on your own this morning because you requested it, Mrs Cartwright, but you must be aware that we shall still need to speak to your husband in due course. There is no need for us to see your son at this stage, unless you think it would serve some useful purpose. Our task is to investigate murder, not child abuse."

She brushed a stray strand of yellow hair away from her forehead impatiently, as if she sought to remove their misapprehensions with the gesture. "I understand that. But there are things about Father Bickerstaffe's abuse of Jason that are different from the other cases. I thought you needed to know about that."

"And without your husband present."

She smiled, that ready smile they were already beginning to think of as natural to her. "When you meet Joe and hear his attitudes, you will understand why we wanted to speak to you without him here."

While the two CID officers looked at each other and tried not to anticipate what was coming (first rule of the training school), she went across to the door and called up the stairs, "Jason? The detectives are here."

There was the sound of a teenager's noisy descent of the stairs before a boy much larger than they expected burst into the room, thrusting out his hand to shake theirs in adolescent gaucherie. "Jason Cartwright," he announced breathlessly. His mother's genes were very obvious in the boy. He had her fair hair and blue eyes, her rounded features and her openness of countenance. But he was already nearly six feet tall, and his plumpness was different from hers; it was puppy fat which was already falling away. In two or three years his face, like his body, would be leaner than it was now, as he stood before them on this bright September morning. "I should really be in school," he said, "but Mum said I could take the morning off to talk to you."

Lucy Blake smiled. Of the three people in the room, she was the nearest in age to the boy, and she felt the appeal of hours stolen from under the noses of the pedagogues. She said, "We're investigating the death of Father Bickerstaffe, not his behaviour at the youth club, Jason. That's why we haven't spoken to the other boys involved in the things that went on at the Sacred Heart – well, we spoke to Thomas Kennedy, but only because his father called him in to see us. However, your mother thought there was a particular reason why we might want to hear what you had to say."

The boy looked at his mother, then back at the two strangers in the room. The speeches he had rehearsed all night refused to come now to his lips when he needed them. He said awkwardly, "Well, it's just that – that Father Bickerstaffe and me – well, it wasn't quite like the other lads."

141

Lucy, who thought she knew now what was coming, spoke hastily, thinking to forestall a harsher reaction from Peach. "Are you telling us that you weren't abused by Father Bickerstaffe?"

"No – well, yes, that's what I'm saying, really, I suppose."

Lucy glanced at Joan Cartwright, who appeared distressed for her son, but perfectly calm in her own demeanour. "Are you telling us that what took place between you was a willing exchange?"

The boy's relief was manifest as he seized on the phrase. "Yes, that's it. A willing exchange. That's exactly it. He didn't compel me into anything. You can't call that abuse, can you?"

"How old are you, Jason?"

"I'm fifteen. Older than all the other boys involved. I knew what I was doing. No one was corrupting me."

"Nevertheless, Jason, if you are under sixteen, the law says you are still a child. And anyone having sexual exchanges with a child is guilty of abuse."

"Then the law is an ass, as Dickens says it is." Jason could not conceal his satisfaction in delivering a quotation newly acquired. "I knew what I was doing and I did it freely."

For the first time since the boy had come into the room, Peach spoke – quietly and with understanding, to Lucy's great relief. "It doesn't much matter what the law says now, Jason. Father Bickerstaffe is dead. We're not here to follow up what happened between the two of you, but to find out anything which might have a bearing on how he died."

Jason nodded, seeming suddenly near to tears. "He was a nice man, really, was Father Bickerstaffe. He wouldn't have hurt anyone. Wouldn't – wouldn't have forced himself on anyone who put up any real resistance. But I know he shouldn't have interfered with those children. I'm not stupid."

"No, I can see that, Jason. But you're saying that what he did with you was different from whatever he did with the others."

"Yes, I am. Whatever the law says. I know I'm gay, you see, so I knew just what I was doing."

He had announced his message at last, as he had been determined he would. He glanced at his mother and received a little nod of acknowledgement. Peach studied him for a moment, deflating the drama of his announcement, waiting to bring him back to the matter in hand. "All right, Jason. Your sexual preferences are not our concern, now that Father Bickerstaffe is dead. What we need to know is anything at all which might have a bearing on that death. I'm sure you know by now that he was murdered."

"Yes. Ten days before his body was found in that river. I've read all about it in the papers. Killed in cold blood."

That was the boy's own addition to the scanty facts published, though it was almost certainly true. They imagined him watching the television news, scanning the newspapers for every scrap of information about the last hours of the man he now romanticised as his dead lover. And in that moment of silence, they clearly heard the sound of a vehicle pulling on to the drive outside.

Jason was at the window in a flash, looking in horror at the white van with 'Cartwright Glass' boldly lettered upon its side. "It's Dad!" he said unnecessarily. "I knew he wouldn't be able to keep away."

His mother tried to calm him with her ready smile. "He didn't know the CID were coming here this morning. He's home for an early lunch, that's all. You'd better let me handle this now. You've said all you wanted to say."

But before the boy could leave the room his father entered, as abruptly as a fireball. "What the hell's going on here? You lot were supposed to be coming this afternoon. I wanted to be here to know what was being said."

He was bristling with fury. Lucy saw Percy preparing to counter-bristle, but fortunately Joan Cartwright got in first. "I invited them here, Joe. In fact, I asked them specially to come this morning. You'd have had your say, in due course. Detective Inspector Peach made it clear at the outset that they'd want to speak to you later, whatever was said now."

"And just what has been said? I suppose this daft twit has been telling you he's as queer as a coot? Stupid young bugger!"

Before Jason could come back at him, his mother said sharply, "I think you should get off to school, now, Jason. You've missed most of the morning already."

For a moment, it looked as if the boy would argue. Then he turned and moved out of the room with the same strange mixture of grace and awkwardness with which he had entered it. He paused momentarily as he passed his father to stare down defiantly into the older man's angry face from no more than eighteen inches. Joe Cartwright glared in frustration at the blank face of the door for a moment after it had closed upon his departing son. Then he whirled and said, "I want to know everything the boy's said. I'm entitled, as his father."

Peach was more in his element with this truculence. "You're entitled to nowt, as a matter of fact. We haven't conducted any formal interview, and if we had there was a responsible adult present with Jason. Anyway, he didn't tell us much. Just said he was gay. That he was a willing party in whatever went on with Father John Bickerstaffe."

Fermenting his anger, thought Lucy Blake, knowing that a man carried away by his emotions might reveal more than a calm one. If that was Peach's intention it certainly worked. Joe Cartwright shouted, "That's bollocks! Jason's a child, and that bloody priest led him astray. Hanging's too good for the likes of him!"

Peach wondered how often he had heard that vehement cliché, from police and public in almost equal measures. Playing this fish was going to be too easy to give him much satisfaction. "You sound like a man who's quite pleased that Bickerstaffe is dead, Mr Cartwright."

"Too right I am. World's well rid of anyone who corrupts the young like he did."

"You think he tried to corrupt your son?"

"Course he did. And now the silly young bugger thinks he's queer. He'd have been right as rain without that priest."

"Jason says not. He says he'd decided he was gay before he had any sexual dealings with Father Bickerstaffe."

"What bloody Jason needs is a bloody good hiding – pardon my French." He glanced first at his silent wife and then at the impassive young face of Lucy Blake, then addressed his words to Peach in what sounded almost like an appeal. "He'd be chasing skirt like any other fifteen-year-old if it wasn't for the slimy hands of that bloody priest."

Peach smiled. An open, innocent, conciliatory smile. To anyone who knew him, it would have been a danger signal, but Joe Cartwright did not. Percy said, "It's not always as simple as that, Mr Cartwright, as I think you realise really. It may not be easy being gay, but not many people now would think of it as an affliction."

"Gay!" Cartwright wrinkled first his nose and then his whole face in disgust. "What a bloody word! Queer, we always called

145

those buggers, and queer they bloody are, if you ask me. No son of mine's going to grow up to be a poof, if I've anything to do with it."

"Unfortunately, you may not have. Who do you think killed Father John Bickerstaffe, Mr Cartwright?"

Joe was shaken by the sudden change of tack, but too far into his theme to see where it was leading him. "How the hell should I know? Someone whose kid was interfered with, if you ask me."

"Which I did. And you've just told us how you think Jason was interfered with. And it's interesting that you seem to be more angry about it than anyone else we've met. That would make you a leading suspect, wouldn't it?"

Peach's smile was blander than ever, his face at its most open and enquiring. Joe Cartwright, realising too late where his fury had led him, said, "It might. And I'm still glad the bugger's dead. But I didn't kill him."

Lucy Blake flicked open her notebook, poised the tiny gold ball-point above it. "Where were you on the afternoon and evening of the twentieth of August, Mr Cartwright?"

He looked at her as if amazed that an attractive young woman should be turning the knife like this in the wound which Peach had made. "Can't remember, just like that, can I? That's getting on for three weeks ago."

Peach smiled a more threatening smile, the sort that Torquemada might have admired in one of his apprentice torturers. "Eighteen days ago, Joe. Take as much time as you like. When you come up with a story, we'll note it, then check it out. Routine, it's called."

The glazier looked at him as if he would have liked to hit him. It was Joan Cartwright who said nervously, "You were over at Lytham, Joe. You were there for the whole week

146

before the Bank Holiday weekend. That cafe that was having the conservatory put on to make extra space."

"Not a cafe. A pub-restaurant. But she's right: I was glazing an extension they'd had put on to their dining room. It took me the whole of that week – they wanted it open for the Bank Holiday trade, so I had to finish it. Bloody hot work it was, too, in the sun we had that week."

Peach looked at him evenly, watching for any flick of nervousness over the reddish features. "So you were there on the afternoon DS Blake asked you about, that of Thursday the twentieth of August?"

"I told you. I was there all week. Working late to get the work finished, wasn't I, Joan?"

His wife's blonde, blue-eyed head nodded, her habitual smile flowing back in her relief. "He was late home every night that week. Seven thirty or eight, it would be. And that would include Thursday."

He gave them the name of the pub in Lytham St Anne's readily enough, seemingly only too anxious for them to check him out and clear him. Lucy Blake said, "And where were you on that day, Mrs Cartwright?"

She looked surprised that she should even be asked to account for herself, and her husband was preparing to bluster protectively when she said coolly, "I was here on that day. Jason and I had our meal early, without waiting for Joe to arrive home. We knew he'd be late, and Jason was going out with a friend. My son will be able to confirm that for you, I'm sure."

Peach said courteously, "Thank you. The more people we can eliminate from our enquiries, the better, from our point of view." He whirled suddenly upon Joe Cartwright. "So, are you going to tell us now who you think killed Father Bickerstaffe, Joe?"

For the second time in three minutes, the stocky man looked like a middleweight who had been stopped in his tracks by a body blow. "How the hell should I know?"

"Oh, come on, now. You just said first that you were glad he was dead and secondly that you thought the likeliest killer was someone whose child had been abused. You must have been thinking about it – assuming you don't actually know, that is."

"Of course I don't know! And if I did, I wouldn't bloody tell you. That bastard had it coming to him!"

"On which note of co-operation, we shall leave you. For the moment. I would remind you that if you think of anything or find out anything which bears on the case in the next few days, it is your duty to report it to us immediately. Ask for DI Peach at Oldford nick and I'll be round here like a hungry whippet."

Peach waved to the blonde head of Joan Cartwright and the thunderous face beside it as Lucy drove him away.

Twelve

Percy Peach rolled on to his back and looked at the crack in the ceiling. "I still can't believe it," he said.

Lucy Blake, her head resting comfortably upon his arm, followed his gaze. "It's there all right," she said. "Nothing to worry about, though. A bit of filler and a coat of paint and you wouldn't even see it."

"Not the ceiling, you daft haporth! You and me, I mean."

"Oh, that. Well, I can't quite believe it either. Perhaps I'm just sleeping with my boss to get on in my chosen profession."

Percy grinned up at the ceiling. "If tha were serious about that, tha'd be in bed with Tommy Bloody Tucker. Now that *would* be a fate worse than death, lass."

Lucy Blake smiled, stirring her legs beneath the duvet, settling the back of her neck more comfortably into the crook of his arm. She liked it when he thee'd and tha'd her, called her 'lass' and 'daft haporth'. She hadn't been called that since she was a little girl with her granddad, and you hadn't been able to buy a halfpennyworth of anything since long before she was born. But the Lancashire speech was a sort of intimacy between them, setting off this most unexpected alliance from their workaday selves and the squalid side of the world which they inhabited there.

"Tha'd better not tell thy mother what th'art up to," said Percy. "She'll have thee home and locked up if tha does."

Lucy giggled, and the tremor ran through her naked body in a way which had a disturbing but wholly predictable effect upon Percy Peach. "Tha'rt right there and no mistake, Sir Jasper!" she said. She wondered indeed when she was going to tell her mother about this. A relationship with a divorced man, ten years her senior. It wouldn't sound too good to a mother who lived in a country village and clung to the ways of an older, more ordered world. And no mention of marriage, as yet. That was as much her choice as Percy's: she wasn't sure yet where this attachment was going, though she knew that for both of them it was more serious than they pretended.

"So who do you think killed our priest?" she said, thrusting away thoughts of her mother and stretching lazily against the cool sheet.

"You choose your moments!" said Percy, struggling to control an insistent manhood. He sought her hand, entwined his fingers in hers resolutely to prevent them straying to more exciting regions. "I used to think about the Rovers to try to slow down lustful thoughts. Now it has to be work!"

"I know who you'd like our killer to be."

"And who would that be, oh mind-reader?"

"Charles Courcey, MP and Junior Minister in Her Majesty's Government."

"Ex-MP. And ex-Junior Minister. And if you ask me, Her Majesty is well rid of that bugger. But you're right, if we could pin it on Charles Courcey, I'd be delighted. Not that I bear the obnoxious sod any ill will, of course."

"And not that you'd like to see Thomas Tucker announcing the arrest of a senior Mason."

Percy's grin became seraphic. "Ee, that would be wonderful,

lass, wouldn't it? Reet grand, that would be! But life's not like that. The slimy sod's got an alibi for that Thursday night. He was in London, he says, waiting for a vote in the House. But he's not the kind who'd do his own dirty work, anyway, is Charles de Poshboots Courcey. If he was involved, he'd have some other daft bugger putting the cord round poor old Bickerstaffe's neck. But if he gave the orders, we'll have him, however long it takes."

"But what had he to gain by killing the priest?"

"Ah! We've clarified that, my pretty one. Whatever his weakness for boys, Bickerstaffe seems to have been as horrified by the hardcore child pornography photographs that Courcey sent him as the rest of us. He was about to blow the gaffe on the paedophilia ring that Courcey and his friends were running. That sturdy lady Martha Hargreaves didn't let that fellow into the presbytery to retrieve the letter Courcey had written to Bickerstaffe, but we already had it. Evidence, that letter will be, if we ever bring Lord Snooty to court. Dying breed, the spinster-housekeeper, more's the pity."

"Unlike the spinster-policewoman."

"Ah! Now they have different virtues altogether." Percy succumbed to temptation and shifted his hand to a softer and more intimate area. "If you're going to go through the rest of the suspects, I'll just hold on here for a bit, lass."

"A bit's all you're capable of, Squire Peach, at your advanced stage of life," said Lucy. She turned cautiously to deny him access. "I hope our killer doesn't turn out to be Kate Maxted."

"Don't know her. Didn't see her, you went on your own." Percy's voice was muffled by a rounded shoulder, his mind not on the conversation but on the activities of his exploratory hand and fingers.

"She's a feisty lady, Kate. I liked her. And don't do that, I'm trying to concentrate on the case." She shut her legs, suddenly and with amazing strength. Percy's cry was a mixture of pain, surprise and pleasure. He withdrew his hand, slowly and reluctantly. "Eh, but you *are* strong, lass! And in the most unexpected places, too."

"Just concentrate, please, DI Peach! Kate Maxted: single mother; four children between seven and fourteen, the eldest of whom, Wayne, was assaulted by Bickerstaffe. No husband around, and no maintenance for the children from him. She lives in a terraced house in Primrose Bank, clean but very basic. She's obviously dependent on financial support from Social Services."

"She'd be Tommy Bloody Tucker's chief suspect, then. Primrose Bank and on the social means criminal, to Tommy. Bright enough to have planned this killing, is she, your Kate Maxted?"

"Not mine. And just keep your hands still and let me think, will you? Yes, she's a bright woman. Battered by life with a brutal husband, trying to cope with four children on her own with no money, but bright enough. Proud of it, even: she made a point of telling me she could have stayed on at school to do A levels. And it's not just book learning: you can't survive as she has without learning a lot about the mechanics of living."

"Opportunity?"

"I asked her about Thursday and Friday, because we still didn't know then that he'd died on the Thursday evening. She'd no alibi for the Friday, but that doesn't matter now. She says she was at home with the kids at teatime on the Thursday – we'd have to question them to confirm that, but she didn't strike me as the type to let her kids lie for her. Besides, she's shrewd enough to know that four children will soon contradict themselves if you ask them to tell lies for you."

"So she didn't do it herself. What's the chance of her having a partner in crime to do the dirty deed?"

Lucy was silent for so long that he began to divert himself with the charms of a smoothly rounded buttock. Then she said, "There might be a man around – or even a woman, I suppose. There was nothing I could put my finger on, but I got the impression there might be someone."

"Ee, I do like something I can put my finger on, lass," said Percy, and attempted to demonstrate his liking.

She dug her nails forcefully into his wrist, "You might have your finger cut off, if it makes me lose my thread. Let's agree that Kate Maxted might be involved in some way, and can't be eliminated without further investigation. Your turn now. Let's have your views on Keith and Pat Hanlon."

"Ee, lass, but you're a hard taskmaster! Well, they're good Catholics, with all that that implies. I was brought up on people like the Hanlons, until I strayed on to the primrose path and ended up with a scarlet woman like you."

"Are you saying that makes them less likely to have killed? Their duty to observe the fifth commandment? 'Thou shalt not kill' and all that?"

"By no means. Murder recruits its servants everywhere – must remember to quote that to Tucker, it sounds rather good. Not biblical, but my very own. I always suspect people who quote scripture at me and talk about their Christian duty. Pat Hanlon did both: 'Vengeance is the Lord's, not any man's', she told her husband. I distrust people who try to live their lives by dogma, just as I distrust politicians who parrot slogans at me."

"I hope it's not the Hanlons, though. They seemed a genu-inely close-knit family, very attached to their children."

"Agreed. Unfortunately, that doesn't necessarily make them less likely to kill. They were probably more outraged and distressed by what happened than anyone. Like Kate Maxted they have four children, but in their case only the eldest is a boy."

She nodded, arresting Percy's straying hand and taking it tightly in hers again. "And that's Jamie, the lad who was assaulted. Their first-born, and their cherished only son. Would that mean the abuse hit them even harder?"

"It might. As might the fact that they were the last to expect what was going on. There was a kind of innocence about them: they couldn't believe a priest would do such things, until the evidence was set before their eyes. Jamie was an altar boy, who regularly served Mass for Bickerstaffe. It must have made the betrayal even more shocking and their bitterness even deeper."

"Do you think there was enough bitterness for them to have killed Bickerstaffe?"

"I don't know." Percy rose a little in the bed, propped himself on one elbow, reluctantly forced himself to consider the case. "That suffocatingly pious atmosphere, that notion that a priest defiling his cloth was almost more shocking than his defiling of their son, took me back to my boyhood. I didn't think there were households like that any more, at once so pious, so genuinely caring for their children, and so blind to the world outside their religion. I found their piety obfuscating things for me, masking what they really felt."

"I know what you mean. I felt there were naked human emotions like hatred seething underneath the standard pious phrases. But the Hanlons weren't so innocent that they didn't expect to be questioned as suspects. They had their stories ready about what they were doing on that Thursday afternoon. I'm sure that they'd discussed it before we arrived."

"I'm sure of that too. But it doesn't make them more likely to be guilty. Even the innocent know that they're likely to be questioned, so they think about what they were doing at the time of a murder. By the time we saw them, the papers had printed the news that Bickerstaffe had been dead for about ten days before the body was found, so they knew that that Thursday was a key day."

"And if we accept what they say, they were nowhere near Downton Hall. But of course, they're alibi-ing each other from the time when Keith Hanlon says he left that solicitors' office in Preston. That's been checked out, by the way. He left there around half-past four."

"If it was the Hanlons, they're both involved. It's difficult to see two such pious buggers taking the law into their own hands and killing a man. But there's no doubt that Bickerstaffe's treachery hit them very hard – perhaps harder than it hit any of the others. Good Catholic families stick together – 'The family that prays together, stays together', they used to tell me when I had to recite the rosary as a child. Perhaps the parents also take vengeance together. But perhaps that's also my own prejudice against a religion I no longer accept."

"Percy Peach with hang-ups! I'm finding more hidden depths all the time."

Percy snuggled down again. "So am I, if you'll only let go of my hand. I'll soon show you—"

"David Kennedy. What about him?"

"Ooh, you are firm, lass! And so am I. If you'll just feel here you'll soon see just how firm—"

"DI Peach! Behave yourself. Tell me whether you see David Kennedy as a murderer."

Percy sighed. "All right. He's a real passion-killer anyway, is that Kennedy. Can't see him in bed with a randy redhead, doing her a bit of good from the charity of his heart. Ow! You know, your elbows are really sharp, lass. Not like the rest of you at all. You should be careful with them. David Kennedy, then. A Puritan, if ever I saw one. And Puritans who go over the top always go further than other people. Look at Cromwell. When you were educated by the Irish Christian Brothers, you were always being made to look at Cromwell."

"All right, so Kennedy's a Puritan. And Percy Peach doesn't like Puritans. Is that all you have to offer about him as a suspect?"

"No. He's an older Dad than all the others. Nearer to a grandfather, in age: fifty-seven, I think. His wife left him for a younger man and he's bringing up two teenage boys on his own. All stress factors. And he's by nature a very intense man, is David Kennedy. And intensity often spills over into violence. You saw how he wanted to hit me when I riled him a bit."

"But that's no guide. If everyone who wanted to hit Percy Peach was a murderer, the prisons couldn't contain them."

Percy smiled at the ceiling and stretched ecstatically; Lucy retained a firm grip on his hand. "Flattery will get you anywhere, my girl. But there's more. Kennedy doesn't like the Catholic Church – in fact I'd say he hates it to the point of unbalance. He associates it with his wife and her desertion. He couldn't wait for his boys to reject the religion. Think how savage he must have felt when a representative of that faith assaulted his younger son. Curiously enough, I think the fact that the Hanlons are obsessed with Catholicism and the fact that David Kennedy hates everything about it makes

156

both of them more likely to have resorted to violence when Bickerstaffe abused their boys."

"So you think they're the strongest candidates?"

Percy protested. "You're putting me on the spot now." The notion suggested a lascivious move, and he made a determined effort to reach another spot, but was foiled by a resolute police officer. He sighed. "I don't know who would be my strongest candidate, to be honest. I do know that I don't really want it to be either of them. I think the Hanlons are a close family, with loving parents struggling to give their kids standards in a difficult world. And David Kennedy may not be my type, but I think he's a bit of a hero too, in his own way, though I'd never let him know I thought that. He's doing his best for two sons who may not always appreciate his efforts, and has done for years. If we had more parents like Kennedy and the Hanlons, there'd be less crime for us to struggle with."

Lucy found herself wondering just what sort of parent Percy Peach might make. That was a dangerous area, and she said hastily, "That only leaves the Cartwrights, among our major suspects. What did you make of them?"

"Funny lot. But not so unusual really, I suppose. A protective mother; a fifteen-year-old who announces he's gay; a Dad who has never expected it, probably never even thought about it, and can't accept it."

"And a mother who is so scared that her husband will incriminate himself that she tries to see us on her own with Jason."

"Doesn't necessarily mean she thinks Joe Cartwright did it, though, does it? Might mean that she was just embarrassed by the attitude she knew her husband would take, and thought he'd get less annoyed if we saw him on his own. Of course, she wasn't to know that Percy Peach could make a saint lose his temper, if it suits him."

"I could, couldn't I? You say the nicest things, lass, but I still think you're only after me for my body. I'm going to give up all resistance, in a minute."

She ignored him, knowing his fate and his movements were firmly in her hands. "He's a homophobic, Joe Wainwright. That would upset his judgement, make him capable of going off to kill the man he believes has set his son on the evil path of homosexuality."

"He doesn't like gays, that's certain. Whether you could call it a phobia, likely to upset all rational intelligence, is another matter. But if he really believed that his son wouldn't have been gay without Bickerstaffe's attentions, I agree that might well have driven him to violence. He needs further investigation, does honest Joe Wainwright. But he's not alone in that. There are several alibis that merit close scrutiny. Even according to what his wife says, Joe wasn't in until seven thirty to eight on that Thursday night. Wonder what time he left that pub he was working at in Lytham."

"Do you think we'll ever find the murder weapon?"

"Not a chance, I should think. My guess is that that length of cord has either been burned or is at the bottom of the Ribble or the Hodder. A man who's careful enough to empty a corpse's pockets doesn't leave a cord in his shed."

"Or her shed."

"Correct. I haven't forgotten that a woman like your Kate Maxted could have garrotted an unsuspecting victim as easily as any man. I'm as much a feminist as anyone, when it comes to murder. However, there are some activities for which women are much better fitted than men."

And with one bound, he was free. Or rather with one sudden

wrench of his hands. In the next ten minutes of intense activity, Percy Peach allowed Detective Sergeant Blake, junior to him in rank and age, to have her evil way with him. A determined feminist he, even in the last stages of exhaustion.

Thirteen

S ince the trouble at home, Joe Cartwright was more than ever glad to get to his work as a glazier. You had to concentrate when you were working with glass, or it came back at you. There was no time to think of your domestic problems, of that silly young Jason who thought he was queer and his mother who made things worse by indulging him. There weren't many people in the county who could cut a tricky piece of glass as swiftly and accurately as Joe, and he was proud of that.

Not that his work on that Tuesday morning was stretching his craftsmanship very far. Fitting sealed double-glazed windows into new houses didn't call for a high degree of skill, in Joe's opinion, though the cowboys could still produce a botched job through ignorance and carelessness. It was a bright September morning, but quite sharp: there had been a hint of autumn in the cool air when he had begun his work today. His hands were warmer now, as he applied the mastic to the ready-made windows, sealing the frames against the rains which would pound this western face of the house in the years to come. Joe's face was a picture of concentration, the tip of his tongue appearing at the corner of his mouth as his fingers moulded the long line of mastic along the edge of the frame, then disappearing as he

160

reached the corner, as if it was tied to his thumb by some invisible string.

It wasn't until he had completed the sealing of the window that he caught sight of a reflection of someone behind him in the double-glazed unit, and his activity was suddenly frozen.

"Good job, that! Nice to see a craftsman at work," said Percy Peach.

Joe turned to meet the blandest of smiles beneath the black eyebrows and the bald pate. "It's easy, this. But it pays the bills. And I get the job for the whole site, if this first house is satisfactory. It will be."

"I'm sure it will," said Percy amiably. "You work for some dodgy people, though, Joe."

Joe Cartwright glanced round quickly to make sure the man who had brought him here was not about; Peach hadn't bothered to lower his voice. "Makes no difference to me how Tom Conlon goes about things," Joe said. "I'm self-employed, so I pay my own stamp. So long as I'm paid what we've agreed for the job, I've no complaints. When you work for yourself, you can't afford to turn away work."

They both knew what he was talking about. T.J. Conlon, whose name Peach had seen on the board as he came on to the site, was a man who employed casual building workers 'on the lump', without paying insurance or declaring them as workers to the taxman. It was illegal, but it was an abuse which was difficult to keep pace with in an industry like building, where the work moved from site to site and the workforce expanded and contracted almost weekly.

Peach nodded, studying his man, noting his uneasiness once his hands had stopped working at his trade. "We checked your story about Lytham, Joe. Most helpful, that publican was. Says you left early on that Thursday – round about four thirty. Said you were going to collect materials, apparently. But strangely enough, he doesn't remember you arriving with anything much on the Friday morning."

"That's where I went. He's right – I remember now. I collected some small stuff, for a partition I was making in the restaurant. Beading, and a bit of stained glass for the top panels."

"Strange that the man who was employing you doesn't remember you bringing those things on the Friday. Who supplied you? Warners, was it?"

Warners was the biggest wholesale timber supplier in Brunton. "That's right, yes. The beading, that is. I had the stained glass in my garage at home."

"And yet no one at Warners remembers seeing you that day. And their computer records show no purchase by Joe Cartwright in that week." Percy's smile widened; his face swam a little before Cartwright's frightened eyes, until he thought that when his tormentor finally went away, that white-toothed smile would remain to mock him, like the Cheshire Cat's.

"They must have got it wrong. It was only a bit of beading. I reckon they forgot to ring it up to my account."

"No, Joe. We both know they didn't. Just as we know that a self-employed man wouldn't lose two or three hours' work to pick up a bit of beading. I think you should tell me where you were between four thirty and seven thirty on that day. Unless you were up in the Ribble Valley killing Father John Bickerstaffe, that is, when you'd be better to wait until you have your brief sitting beside you at the station." Peach sucked his bottom lip up into the gaps where his upper canine teeth should have been, looking for a moment like a pike swallowing its prey, and then resumed his Cheshire Cat mode.

"I didn't kill bloody Bickerstaffe."

"Convince me, Joe."

"I can't. I was thinking about our Jason on that Thursday, and I just couldn't get my head round it. It was only the night before that he'd told me this rubbish about being gay, and I couldn't think what to do about it. Eventually I knew I couldn't concentrate well enough to work any more – I was starting to make mistakes. I went and sat in a big pub in Lytham and tried to work out what to do. I – I was thinking of writing to one of these agony aunts for advice, if you must know. I sat with a bit of paper and a pencil and tried to put together a letter."

"And was this cry for help published and answered?"

"Of course it wasn't! I never got as far as making up a letter. The more I tried, the dafter it seemed to me."

"So there's no evidence to support this latest story? No crumpled sheets in the depths of your pockets or the back of your van?"

"No. I never was much good at writing stuff down. I slung what I'd done down the bog in the pub."

"Of course you did, Joe. And no doubt the pub was crowded, and no one will remember a man with a pint and a pencil in a corner."

Wainwright looked more and more miserable. "They won't. It was a big pub in the middle of Lytham – I can't even remember the name of it. But it's open all day, and there were a couple of coach parties in. I don't suppose anyone will remember me."

"I don't suppose they will, Joe, no. Probably not worth our time checking. But if you think of a better story, do let me know. I collect unlikely tales."

Joe Cartwright's fear was right. Peach's smile lingered vividly in his mind's eye, long minutes after the man himself was gone.

*　　*　　*

Half an hour later on that Tuesday morning, 8th September, Superintendent Tucker gave Detective Inspector Peach his overview of the case. He had forbidden the taking of notes, and Percy sat on the edge of his chair, leaning forward with an air of such intense concentration that Tucker was in constant danger of losing the thread of his already scanty thoughts.

"My advice would be to concentrate on this Maxted woman. She's bound to be pretty desperate, living off the Social Services, with four children round her skirts."

"Yes, sir. Good point that, sir." Peach, wrinkling his forehead to show how earnestly he treasured this banality, wondered how long it had been since women like Kate Maxted moved round the house in skirts. "Handy woman with a garrotting wire, Kate would be, I shouldn't wonder."

Tucker's face fell. His conventional mind still balked at the thought of a woman tightening a wire round the throat of an unsuspecting victim. Though he had long since ceased to read anything except newspapers and official documents, he had been brought up on Dickensian heroines, and the images of Agnes Wickfield and Little Nell still dominated his ideas of young womanhood. The notion of any woman being the agent of violent death remained difficult for him, despite thirty years of marital experience. He said uncertainly, "Don't rush into anything, Peach."

"No, sir." Peach nodded firmly several times, as if to drive that thought firmly into his dull brain, as if he had been contemplating a headlong leap over Beachy Head until he was checked by his charitable superior. Then he leaned forward. "There seems to be some possibility that there's a new man in her life," he said darkly.

"Ah! You think she's going to remarry?"

164

"Couldn't say that, sir. Women like Kate Maxted have a habit of living over t'brush, as we say in these parts." He was gratified to see his chief looking suitably baffled. Served him right for coming from Cheshire. "No sign of a man in the house, but we're following it up."

"Well, do it then. Don't let the grass grow under your feet. This is a murder enquiry, you know. I've got a media conference lined up for tomorrow and I'm looking to you and the team to produce results."

"Yessir!" Peach almost sprang to attention, but settled eventually for sitting bolt upright in his chair. He spoke rapidly now, with an air of irresistible urgency. "There's an older man whose wife has left him with two boys, the younger of whom was assaulted. David Kennedy; very intense man. There's a very pious Catholic couple, Keith and Pat Hanlon, whose eldest child was assaulted. There's Joe and Joan Cartwright, whose son says he's gay and was a willing party, but was technically assaulted because he's only fifteen. Joe Cartwright thinks he was led astray by Bickerstaffe and wouldn't be queer without him."

Tucker reeled before the machine-gun verbal delivery of this trio. "Following all this up, are you?"

"Yes, sir. Of course, sir. The team is on it now, sir."

"I should think they are. I shall need an up-to-date written summary of your progress tomorrow morning."

"Yes, sir. Of course, sir. Ready for the media conference. It's good of you to keep us out of the limelight so that we can get on with the detection, sir."

Tucker looked at him suspiciously, but found Peach's eyes upon that spot a foot above his head which seemed perennially to fascinate the Inspector. "Well, if you've nothing else to report, you'd better be getting on with it."

165

Percy sprang to his feet and picked up his chair to return it whence he had brought it. He positioned its feet with extreme care, as if it was important that every detail of the bleak decor of the Head of CID's room should be preserved. It was the moment for his last turn of the knife. "Your friend Charles Courcey's turned up," he said.

"I don't know where you ever got this idea that Courcey was a friend of mine, Peach. I certainly never gave you that impression."

Not half you didn't, thought Percy. You were shit scared of doing anything about him, until he disgraced himself publicly. "No, sir. I must have picked up a wrong idea. Him being a big pot in the Masons and so on."

"I don't know how many times I have to tell you, Peach, that my Masonic activities are nothing at all to do with my work in the police force."

Except that they got you the chair you sit in, you great twit, thought Percy. "Yes, sir. I'll try to remember that. Anyway, Charles Courcey was arrested last night by the Child Pornography Unit as he re-entered the country. He's being charged today and held in Wormwood Scrubs. We need to interview him in connection with our Bickerstaffe murder. I thought you might like to go down to London and do it yourself, sir. Being as you're in charge of the case." Nominally, that is, O Prattus Maximus.

"Oh, I'm far too busy for that, Peach. You'll have to do it yourself." Tucker brightened. Being as usual months behind with the station gossip, he thought it would irritate Peach to be saddled with a woman officer for a long journey. "Take Detective Sergeant Blake with you. Be good experience for her."

And me, thought Percy. A night of passion at police expense. Nirvana. He said dolefully, "If you say so, sir."

*   *   *

It was not more than five minutes after Percy Peach had left Joe Wainwright that another man stole silently to his side.

Joe was trying hard to become engrossed in his work again after Peach's disturbing visit, but this man did not wait to be noticed. "That was the filth, Joe, that came a-calling. What did he want?"

It was a gentle Dublin brogue, and Joe knew who the speaker was before he turned to confront him. Tony Reilly, a big, raw-boned Irishman with a small black beard, great strength and a reputation for wildness. A hod-carrier on the site; a skilled carpenter, capable of more highly paid work than humping bricks, but unable for some reason to obtain it; a man working for Tommy Conlon on the lump because he could get nothing better. Joe Wainwright said cautiously, "It was a CID man, yes. Detective Inspector Peach, if you want his name. Cocky little bugger. He's looking into the murder of that priest who assaulted the boys up at the Sacred Heart."

Reilly nodded. "That's him. He's been to the other parents as well, you know. But not to my Kate. It was a girl who went to see her. Young, sturdy, reddish hair, Kate said. She told Kate she was a Detective Sergeant."

Joe nodded. "Sounds like the one who came to see us with Peach. Blake, she said her name was. Quite a looker – you'd never have guessed she was a policewoman. And she scarcely looked old enough to be a CID sergeant, but then they look younger all the time to me."

"What did Peach want with you today?" asked Reilly.

Joe paused, wondering how much he should tell this man, who seemed to carry the menace of violence with him like a garment. He'd seen Reilly on Sunday mornings at church, and for the last few days he'd watched him humping huge numbers of bricks about the site. But the Irishman must have a dubious past, or he wouldn't be reduced to working for Tommy Conlon on the lump. In the end, the need to confide in the face of the pressure being exerted by the police was too strong for Joe, and he said, "He came here asking about my alibi for the time when that bastard Bickerstaffe was murdered."

"And when was that?"

Reilly was eager, too eager, with his question and Joe said quickly, "What's it to you, Tony?"

Reilly glanced automatically to right and left, with the hunted air of a man who has suffered and wishes to make sure that he is not overheard. "It's my Kate. She's a suspect too, you know. They've already questioned her, and from what you say they'll be back. I want to protect her."

Wainwright looked up into the face of the big Irishman. A selfish thought told him that if he could divert some of Peach's suspicion elsewhere, that could only help him. But his overwhelming feeling was one of relief. There were others who were glad to see Bickerstaffe dead, others in the frame for this killing, as well as him. He felt a common cause with this rough fellow against the police machine. Joe said slowly, "They're interested in the evening of twentieth August, eleven days before the body was found."

"The girl asked Kate about that Thursday. And the Friday as well."

"Well, from what they said to us, it sounded as though they were pretty sure that Bickerstaffe was killed on that Thursday evening."

The two men looked at each other for a moment, each trying to assess how much the other knew about his movements on that day. Then Joe, attempting to lighten the tension, said, "Serious, are you, with Kate Maxted?"

He had thought it was a safe question, but he saw the big man's fists clench at his sides and feared for a moment that they would move to hit him. Then the Irishman said, "Yes, we're serious. But the police don't know about me and Kate, and I want it to stay like that."

Joe said hastily, "It will, Tony, it will! I won't tell anyone, now I know you don't want me to. And certainly not the police."

Reilly stared at him for a moment, breathing heavily, then nodded abruptly. "Remember that, Joe. It's the Social, you see. They come prying round Kate's place if they think there might be another man around."

"Yes. I see that. And you can be sure I won't tell anyone, least of all the police." Joe Wainwright had the feeling that the Social wasn't the real reason for Reilly's command of secrecy, that it had been added as an attempt to justify his reaction. But he had more sense than to speculate about the real reason.

He didn't know a lot about Tony Reilly, but he knew he was not a man to cross without risking violence.

Fourteen

Percy Peach was enjoying himself. He liked busting people's alibis. He liked even more confronting people to tell them their stories had been busted. Best of all, he liked to confront puritanical people like David Kennedy, who prided themselves on telling the truth and never having to deal with anyone as dubious as a policeman.

They were at the huge electrical works which had become the biggest employer in the town since the decline of King Cotton had closed most of the mills. Peach had half-expected that Kennedy's work in the research department would have seen him wearing a white coat, but he was dressed instead in a dark grey suit, well worn and a little out of fashion. Kennedy, Percy reflected, was probably a man without either the money or the inclination to pay much attention to fashion. He had his own office, but it was a tiny cubicle of a room, a sixth of the size of the top-floor office Tommy Tucker afforded himself at Brunton nick.

That thought brought with it a grudging sympathy for Kennedy, who looked in his anxiety even older than his fifty-seven years: his lean face was drawn and his grey eyes looked very tired under the silvering hair. But Peach conjured up the anxious face of the man's thin, bespectacled son Thomas, who had been abused by the priest and had patently feared that it was his father who had extracted the ultimate revenge for that assault.

Kennedy had closed the door carefully behind them on the busy world of the factory and his laboratory. This ensured that, as they sat opposite each other and talked with their feet tucked beneath their chairs, his bony knees almost touched the thicker ones of DI Peach. He said, "What brings you here to my place of work, Mr Peach? I thought we said all we had to say to each other on Sunday."

"Did you, sir?" Percy's surprise was manifest, his black eyebrows arching high into his bald dome. "Oh, I didn't think so. Not by a.long chalk. But then, I don't suppose you'd be familiar with our methods."

"I would not, I'm happy to say."

"Well, we're thorough, you see, sir. Plodding, but thorough. Unimaginative sometimes, I shouldn't wonder, but methodical."

"Really. One would question that sometimes, in view of the number of serious crimes which go unsolved."

"You might well wonder about that; indeed, I do myself, sometimes. Still, our clear-up rate on murders isn't bad round here, not bad at all. I don't suppose you're a betting man, sir, but you might do well to put a tenner or two on us finding out who killed Shirtlifter Bickerstaffe by the end of the week, if you get the chance."

Kennedy indicated his contempt with an acerbic smile. "You still haven't seen fit to tell me why you're disrupting my work schedule today."

"No. Well, let's put that right, then. When people spin us a tale, we like to check it out. That's part of our method."

"And whose tale are you checking out today?"

"Yours, Mr Kennedy, as you've no doubt guessed by now.

171

And it's been found wanting." Percy didn't need to add 'I'm glad to say'. His beaming smile, stretching further across his round face than David Kennedy would have thought possible, was more eloquent than words.

The scientist licked his lips, found them surprisingly dry, and said, "You're saying that something I told you is wrong? I doubt whether it is, but until you enlighten me about what I said, I shan't be able to recall—"

"Your story about where you were at the time when Father Bickerstaffe was being murdered. That's what's wrong, Mr Kennedy. It's always of great interest to us when someone lies about their whereabouts at a time like that." Peach's smile had vanished as abruptly and completely as it had arrived. His coal-black eyes seemed to be peering into the older man's very soul. "You said you were late home that evening, that you didn't arrive until half-past seven because you were detained here by a meeting of the research staff. No such meeting took place on that particular Thursday: I've confirmed that with your colleagues in the last half-hour."

"Then there wasn't any meeting. It must have slipped my mind that we didn't meet on that particular Thursday – we usually do."

"Slipped your mind, Mr Kennedy? A mind like yours, that prides itself on being precise? It's only just over two weeks ago. I think you can do better than 'slipped your mind', if you try a bit harder."

"I don't care for your tone, Inspector Peach. It sounds to me as if you're accusing me of lying, and—"

"We'll let the court be the judge of your honesty, if it comes to it." Percy's tone was at once curt and disappointed. People who were used to being honest and straightforward rarely made effective liars when forced into it, and Percy preferred the challenge of less synthetic opposition than this. "We'll accept that you weren't home until seven thirty on that day. You'd better tell me where you were between four thirty, which seems to be the last time anyone I've spoken to was aware of you round here, and seven thirty."

Kennedy was looking at Peach's brightly polished black shoes. Everything about this awful little man seemed to be black or white. He kept his eyes on the shoes as he said, "I was here. I was in the laboratory until some time after five, on my own. Then I made myself a mug of tea and sat in this room. I was thinking about what had happened to my son, what long-term effect it might have on Thomas."

"You didn't go out to a pub for a drink? Somewhere where we could check if anyone saw you?"

"I don't drink, Inspector."

No, you wouldn't, you starchy bugger, thought Peach. But you might just have been out in Bolton-by-Bowland, waiting for the man who had done this to your son, the minister whose church you hated almost more than his deed. Perversely, he found himself hoping it had not been so. Kennedy, whatever his personality, had not the qualities of a criminal. But that was the trouble with murder: it made its own rules, driving people who were not normally intemperate to take violent actions under the stress of extreme emotions. Percy looked at the baldness among the thinning grey hair of the head cast down before him and spoke more quietly. "Think carefully, please, Mr Kennedy; I assure you it's in your own interest. Is there anyone – a cleaner, perhaps, or one of the security staff – who could confirm that you were here during those hours?"

Kennedy thought, or gave the appearance of thinking. "No. I don't remember seeing anyone. I don't think there was even anyone in the car park when I left. There were only a couple of cars still there at that time."

Peach stood up. "Don't leave the area without letting us know," he said formally.

"With two boys dependent on me? Your guarantee of my whereabouts is Liam and Thomas, Inspector." David Kennedy sounded bitter as well as resigned about the ties his boys had brought to him.

The stress of a murder investigation takes its toll on even the most devoted of couples. The Hanlons were well aware of that on the cool Tuesday evening of the eighth of September.

Pat watched her husband in the bedroom as he went through the pockets of his suits and jackets for what must have been at least the fourth time. He was aware of her attention, and as the futility of his search became more and more apparent, he grew irritated with his wife. "Can't you find anything better to do than watch me?" he rapped at her, his frustration turning as she had known it must upon the nearest target.

She smiled at him, her pale anxiety its own rebuke, and went down to the kitchen and the evening meal for the family. She checked the potatoes, put the cauliflower on to boil, placed the cutlery precisely on the white Formica of the round table beneath the window at the other end of the big kitchen, took the lemon meringue pie out of the fridge and cut it precisely into slices. She smiled her first real smile in hours as she did that: however careful she was, she knew the children would argue about the portions, would know whose turn it was to choose first. If only adult life could be as noisy and carefree as theirs; if only parental problems could be no more important than who got the extra crumbs of a favourite dessert.

Yet even as she went through the mechanics of meal

preparation, hoping in vain that the routine tasks she knew so well would soothe away the pain of her anxiety, she knew that the simplicity of childish life was no more than another illusion. Why else did she and Keith watch Jamie so apprehensively to see what effect that awful business with Father Bickerstaffe was having upon him; why else did they fear for its effect upon the three girls behind him in the family?

She went and called for the children when the meal was ready. They came tumbling into the room, arguing with each other, lifting her a little as usual with their collective energy, their capacity to look forward with lively anticipation to the morrow. Pat wished she could still do that. She looked automatically at Keith when he came down from their bedroom and sat down with his back to the window. He gave her a little shake of the head, then his face twitched with a little spurt of silent indignation that she should still be watching him so closely.

He was quiet during the meal, answering her queries about portions abstractedly, failing to come up with his usual series of questions to the children about what had happened to them in their days at school. The meal seemed to Pat to proceed by conversational fits and starts, with periods of heavy silence punctuated by two of the children speaking at once, but perhaps she was imagining that. She found it increasingly difficult to distinguish between what was real and normal and what was merely the product of her over-active and febrile imagination.

Jamie was also quiet tonight. She was sure at least that she was not imagining that. The fourteen-year-old scarcely spoke as he picked his way through his braised steak, new potatoes and cauliflower, normally his favourite meal. And when the girls' voices shrilled in the ritual dispute over the first choice of the lemon meringue pie, he did not join in, but smiled absently and waited his turn. Almost as quiet, in fact, as his father: Pat caught her son glancing speculatively at Keith as the father of this normally animated family maintained his abstraction from what was going on around him.

Jamie lingered when the girls went off to their rooms, only too anxious to avoid the washing up. Usually Keith directed this task, summoning the family to help him in a rota of impeccable fairness, but tonight Pat and Jamie did the dishes. She was happy as always to be alone with her eldest child and only son, reinforcing that unique intimacy between them that seemed as strong as ever, even as he moved towards the trials of adolescence. Tonight, as they conducted the routine task in diligent silence, she was aware with a mother's intuition that he had something to say to her, and for the first time in many hours her anxiety was subsumed in her curiosity as to what Jamie's concern might be.

It was not until he was drying the last of the crockery that Jamie spoke. He polished the big dish which had contained the steak with elaborate, unnecessary care as he said, "I thought I might go back to serving Mass next week, Mum."

Pat said, "Are you sure you're ready, love? There's no need to prove anything, you know."

"No. But I'd like to. I enjoy serving, being a part of the Mass." He didn't like to add that it made it all go much more quickly, when you had to concentrate hard. You were supposed to enjoy the Mass, to feel the uplifting quality of your worship of the Lord, he knew. But there was enough of the schoolboy in Jamie to find boredom coming easily, to seek for ways of making his time in church pass quickly through involvement.

"Well, that's good. That you want to be involved again, I

mean." The old vague hope that her only son might become a priest, might become a minister in the faith which meant so much to her, prodded again at the back of Pat's mind. "You can go down to St Mary's. They have two masses every morning there, and I'm sure they'd be glad of someone as experienced as you to add to their serving roster."

"I thought I'd go up to the Sacred Heart. It's much more convenient, and Michael said the priest they've got standing in up there at the moment is really nice. Mike's hoping he'll get the job permanently." He saw the look of fear on his mother's face, the desire to protect him which he no longer needed. "It's all right, Mum, it is really. I'm over the shock of all that now."

Even now, Pat thought, they could not refer to what had happened in specific terms. At least, she couldn't: she had a sudden apprehension that Jamie's circumlocutions were a concession to her. She said dully, "Are you sure it's wise to go back so soon? These things have more of an effect than we realise, sometimes."

"Mum, what happened to me was no big deal. Father Bickerstaffe was a sad man, I realise that now. But he didn't really force his attentions on me, once he had to accept that I didn't want them. Much worse has happened to lots of boys at school. I'm lucky living in a family like ours."

So he's been talking about it to the other boys, Pat thought. Exchanging notes on how they've been abused, how far it went. She felt a sharp pang of jealousy at her son's growing up; others were now intruding upon the intimacy with her son which she had for so long thought her own preserve; others were bringing to him news of experiences she could never bring. She forced a smile. "All right then, if you're sure. I'll make enquiries for you, tomorrow, if you like."

"There's no need, Mum. I called in on my way home. Had a little chat with Father Brown – that's the name of the new priest. Only he's not like Chesterton's detective Father Brown: he's young and slim, not middle-aged and tubby." Jamie gave a nervous little laugh, as if to excuse his small treachery in taking this initiative.

"You've worked it all out for yourself, haven't you, love? That's good, though. It'll be nice to see you on the altar again, when I'm at Mass. Makes me feel I've got a personal involvement in what's going on in the worship of Our Lord. I'm sure your Dad feels the same about it, too."

Jamie almost told her that he had only gone back on the altar to fight the boredom of the Mass. He felt again the stifling arms of their religion about him, confining him, making it difficult for him to breathe clear air, like incense in a crowded church. He wanted to be his own man, to find his own ways of belief. Even to discover and explore his own doubts, in due course: the other boys at school were doing that. But you weren't allowed to have doubts, not in this house. He forced a smile for his mother, turned abruptly, and went thankfully away to his room.

The train was speeding southward, even drawing away from the stream of traffic that was breaking the speed limit on the M1. Percy Peach, offered Southern Comfort at the buffet bar, told an uncomprehending barman that that was a contradiction in terms.

"Mum said we could have stayed at my Aunt Amy's," said Lucy Blake when he returned. She was wearing a finely woven wool sweater which matched the ultramarine of her eyes and accentuated the dark red of her hair. It also revealed the curve of her splendid breasts with a pleasing lack of ambiguity. A service to humanity, it was, reflected Percy, taking those out of the constrictions of a police uniform and into the plain clothes of CID. Plain clothes! That was clearly an expression which dated from the days before there was any strong female presence in the service.

"Don't like the sound of Aunt Amy," he said. "Sounds like she'd insist on big bloomers, with elastic at the knee."

"Winceyette, I should think, and double gussets! She's older than Mum."

Percy snuggled closer to her ear, ignoring the tinny overflow from the Walkman of the glazed youth sitting opposite them. "I love it when you talk dirty!" he muttered. "Tell me more about the colour of your smalls."

"They're not winceyette. And that's all I'm telling you for now. These things should come as a surprise."

"I only hope *I* don't come as a surprise," said Percy. "You sexual teasers can go too far, you know. I hope they're very small smalls."

And on that happy tautology, he settled back into his seat and closed his eyes, secure in the anticipation that there was to be much more than teasing this night. Better get a bit of kip while I can, he thought, to husband my resources. There might not be too much sleep later, and he would need to be sharp in the morning to deal with Droopydrawers de Courcey.

He fell into a pleasant alcoholic doze, treasuring the image of Tommy Tucker's idea of punishing him with the company of the delightful DS Lucy Blake.

It is one of the regrettable features of modern life that churches have to be shut up at sundown, to protect them from the larceny and worse which might be visited upon them by the choicer specimens of the society we have produced.

179

The Sacred Heart, being a small enough parish to warrant only a single priest, had a rota of parishioners to perform this task. Keith Hanlon was on this list, but tonight Pat Hanlon had undertaken the task, as her husband was otherwise occupied. She had in truth been glad to get away from Keith, feeling more strongly than ever the strain which had mounted like a tightening wire between them since the announcement of the death of Father John Bickerstaffe.

Dusk dropped in early with autumn approaching. When she slipped into the small, high-roofed church, it was only a few minutes after half-past seven, but it was already almost dark within these high, quiet walls. She locked the door behind her, then went forward to where two candles guttered their last flames in front of the side altar, with its statue of the Sacred Heart of Jesus. She slipped her coin into the collection box, heard it fall unnaturally loud against the metal base as she picked up the slender white candle and lit it from the dying flame of the one lit hours earlier by some anonymous supplicant.

Pat knelt with head bowed before the cheap plaster image, with its hands gesturing towards the exposed heart, surrounded by flames. It would have been a curious and startling image for those not bred in the faith, but Pat Hanlon had known the image of the Sacred Heart for as long as she could remember. A symbol of Christ's love for humanity, it was, an invitation to bring one's troubles to God and be comforted.

But tonight she could gain no comfort in this silent place. Eventually she spoke aloud, through the flickering light of her candle to the impassive statue beyond it. "God forgive me, but I'm glad he's dead! He deserved it, for what he did to my boy. I'm a mother, and he deserved it, for what he did to my boy!"

The blue eyes of the handsome Gentile Christ gazed immovably back at her, and she wished in that moment that she had gone to the other side-altar, where the Mother of Christ in her sky-blue mantle would surely have understood a mother's agony, would surely have condoned a mother's exultation in the death of that agent of the devil's work. She spoke no more words aloud, though she poured forth her heart in explanation of her emotions to the invisible God who lurked behind the plastic figure. Then she retreated into the familiar words of an Our Father and a Hail Mary, recited with great fervour before she stole away, uncomforted.

She knew that she should pray for the quality of forgiveness in herself, so that within her own breast she might forgive the priest Bickerstaffe for what he had done, but she could not yet bring herself to do so. Perhaps forgiveness would be possible, in the days to come. From the rear of the church, she looked back. The other two candles had burnt out now, and her own flame burned its silent worship alone in darkness that was now absolute. She let herself out, locked the church carefully, and walked slowly home, keeping the image of that silent flame in her mind as she went.

It must have been another half-hour before Keith came into the house. She could see from his tortured face that he had found nothing, but for form's sake she had to ask him, "Did you find it?"

"No. It was hopeless, as you said it would be. A needle in a haystack. And I wasn't even sure where I might have dropped it."

She didn't want to voice the thought she knew they both had, but it forced itself out. "If you'd dropped it anywhere obvious, the police might have found it by now. They do searches, I think."

He nodded. "I'm sure they do. But they haven't been back to us. All the signs are that they believe our story. Perhaps they've even arrested someone, by now." But he didn't look as though he believed that.

A few minutes later, their youngest daughter, Rosie, came in to say goodnight, tripping with an eight-year-old's clumsy charm into the quiet room. She threw her arms round her father's neck, kissed him with the extravagance of a child who knew that for some reason her bed-time had been forgotten, and said mischievously, "I've got your pen, Daddy."

For a moment Pat thought that Keith was going to hit her, for the first time in her life. Then holding her at arm's length, he said harshly, "Where did you find it, Rosie?"

The girl knew from his voice that something was wrong. "I borrowed it from your desk." She held out her chubby arm with the gold ball-point. "It's got your name on it, Daddy."

He had control of himself now. "That's right. It's a special pen, isn't it? 'Presented to Keith Hanlon'. That's Daddy. When did you borrow it, sweetheart?"

"When I wrote to Aunty Beth."

To thank her for her birthday present: he remembered the note in her round, eight-year-old hand, the words wide apart, the letters carefully joined. Six weeks and more ago. "Where did you find it now?"

"In my toy box. Under Little Teddy. He'd been hiding it from me, you see."

"Yes. You run along to bed now, there's a good girl. It's long past your time."

There was silence for a long time after the child had gone. They listened to the familiar signs of her undressing in the room over their heads. Pat said, "I'll go and see her down," and Keith knew she was pleased to get out of the room.

When she returned he tried a smile. "I needn't have worried at all. The dratted pen was here all the time."

"Yes. Flipping kids!" It was a saying they had from their own childhood, its origin in Tony Hancock now all but forgotten. She smiled bravely back at him, feeling as drained and relieved as he looked.

In her last thoughts of the evening, just before she fell asleep, Pat Hanlon found herself at last able to regret the death of Father John Bickerstaffe, to pray for mercy upon his immortal soul.

Fifteen

There is something Dickensian about the high-towered entry to Wormwood Scrubs Prison. The whole place has the look of a house of punishment, with its lofty, windowless brick walls and its total concealment of those who are locked into its crowded cells.

Despite the incessant noise of London traffic, the nineteenth century ambience was enhanced by the light mist which hung above the entrance gates when Peach and Blake arrived there, early on the windless morning of the ninth of September. Percy looked at the forbidding entrance appreciatively before they moved to the small pedestrian door to present their credentials. "Should have softened the bugger up nicely, this place," he said. "Wonder if they asked him to slop out this morning."

As they moved towards the room where they would interview Charles Courcey, a series of security gates clanged behind them. Lucy Blake felt her first pang of sympathy for the man they had journeyed two hundred and twenty miles to interview. Paedophiles were the worst of criminals for her, as for most police personnel. But a convicted paedophile had the very worst of the prison system. His life in a place like this would be one of twenty-four hour apprehension about the intentions of his fellow prisoners,

184

who would take as dim a view of his offences as the police and be ruthless in meting out their own kangaroo-court justice.

Courcey presented an abject figure when the warder brought him into the interview room and pointed to the chair opposite Peach and Blake. He wore his own clothes still, but standard prison procedure had deprived him of tie and belt, so that his expensive suit hung loose and ill-fitting about a frame which seemed to have been deprived of its sleekness since they had last seen him only four days earlier, in his constituency rooms in Brunton. There, he had presented himself as an exotic bird moving in a mundane environment; here, he looked like a trussed animal which has already given up all hope of liberty.

If he felt any sympathy for one who had fallen so far, Percy Peach certainly hid it perfectly. "So, Charlie, we meet again. Under very different circumstances, though, eh?"

The former MP winced a fraction at the familiarity with his name, but otherwise continued to look like a beaten cur. "What do you want?" he said wearily.

"A few words about a major crime. We've come a long way to see you, Charlie. All the way from Brunton, which you might just remember."

"I don't know why you've come here. I've nothing more to tell; I've seen enough policemen to last me for the rest of my life in the last thirty-six hours. You've got me stitched up, with the phone tapes, the videos, the letters. I've been very foolish, I admit that. And a few people have let me down. But I've said everything I have to say."

"Don't be too sure about that, Charlie. You and your friends might have tied yourself in knots and presented the Paedophile Squad with an open and shut case for all I know, but I'm not here to talk about that."

Courcey looked up hopelessly at this latest of his tormentors. "What do you want, Peach? You set this in motion, as far as I can see. Isn't it enough for you, all of this?" He lifted his flabby arms six inches and let them flap back hopelessly to his sides, a gesture which took in his environment, his predicament, and his own wretched despondency.

"Afraid not. We're here in connection with a murder investigation," said Peach evenly.

The word had its impact, even here. Courcey looked up at the round face, met the keen black eyes for the first time since he had been led into the room. "I'm not a murderer," he said limply.

"Maybe not. Not personally, that is. But we have reason to think you may have been involved in the murder of Father John Bickerstaffe, Parish Priest of the Sacred Heart Church in Brunton."

"I knew Bickerstaffe. You know all about that. I wrote a foolish letter to him, more's the pity. But I didn't kill him, or cause him to be killed."

"He was going to blow the gaffe on you and your hard-porn circle. You wanted him silenced."

Courcey's haggard face told it all. He wanted to deny the charge, but his will had been broken by the humiliations he had already endured. "All right, I did. We did, not just me. But that doesn't mean I wanted him killed."

Peach pursed his lips. "A fine distinction, that, Charlie, for people with as much at stake as you and your chums. You'll need to convince me."

Courcey's bloodshot, hunted eyes looked from one to the other. He said hopelessly, "And how do I do that? You'll fit me up for whatever you want, now that I've admitted hardcore child pornography. It's not going to matter what I say, is it?"

Lucy Blake spoke for the first time. "It might, if you speak honestly and convince us. But you can't deny that what evidence there is doesn't favour you, Mr Courcey. You dispatched a man to the presbytery at the Sacred Heart to try to recover a letter you'd sent to Father Bickerstaffe, a man who wasn't afraid to hint at violence to get what he wanted, a man who would have got past a less courageous housekeeper than Miss Hargreaves."

Courcey's shoulders lifted and fell with a hopeless resignation. "I don't dispute that. I've already admitted that and a lot of other things. I've even told you we wanted to shut Bickerstaffe up, once we realised that he was planning to talk to the police. But I didn't want him killed. I can't prove that, I can only state it."

Peach shook his head sadly. He said quietly, "I wouldn't be in your shoes, Charlie. Not for all the tea in China and a few Japanese geisha girls as well. You're going down for paedophilia. I know what that conviction means for a prisoner, better than you." Yet even now, Percy wasn't sure this broken hulk of a man would go down. He'd hire the best lawyers. He was as guilty as hell, but the law would maintain he had a right to be defended; it was curious how much more stoutly maintained that right was when there was big money around. There'd be psychiatric reports on Courcey's state of mind; he would state his willingness to undergo treatment with the earnestness of an experienced politician and a public schoolboy's contrition.

Courcey said bitterly, "Thanks for your background information, Peach. I had heard, you know, what happens in prison to – to people like me."

"I'm sure. What I'm getting at, Charlie, is that it might almost be better to go down for murder. Especially if you were not alone in giving the orders to a hitman. Plead mitigating circumstances, nasty company leading you astray, pressure of maintaining a public position; get the headshrinkers in on your side. Throw in the fact that the victim had been abusing lads himself in a minor way and you might get away with five years, with the counsel you're going to employ. Could be out in thirty months, with good conduct, and not a finger laid upon you by the naughty lads in stir with you, as a respectable murderer. It's worth considering, surely?"

For a moment, Courcey looked tempted. Then he said, "That would be all very well, if I'd given any orders for Bickerstaffe to be eliminated like that. But I didn't. I told you, I didn't. I wanted him to keep his mouth shut, because I realised he could do us a lot of damage. But I didn't want him killed."

"So how did you think he was going to be silenced? A priest, even a flawed priest, isn't going to be easy to shut up when he's in the grip of his conscience."

Again that hopeless dropping of the heavy shoulders. "I don't know. I've no experience of these things. I hoped money might do it. I suppose I thought we might be able to bribe him, or perhaps threaten him to frighten him. I know I'm naive in these—"

"Spare us your naivety, Charlie. Keep that for the court: you'll need it. There'll be a statement for you to sign, in due course." Peach was on his feet, ending the interview as harshly and abruptly as he had begun it, nodding to the warder in the corner of the room, watching Courcey intently for any hint of a final revelation. There was none.

Other agencies were at work, however, on the task of illuminating the activities of Charles Courcey, sometime MP and Junior Minister. The charges being compiled against him and his paedophile friends were serious enough for that most

British of taboos, the one on a man's financial dealings, to be breached. This revealed a murky picture, with clarity obscured by a group of accounts in different banks and fundholders, some of them offshore. Money had been transferred into and out of these institutions with the deliberate intention of disguising the real purpose and direction of various payments. Money had passed at bewildering speed between London and Jersey, Spain and Edinburgh.

But by the time DI Peach and DS Blake were back in Brunton that afternoon, it had become clear that a banker's draft of 18th August had transferred five thousand pounds by a roundabout route from the funds of Charles Courcey to the account of a known hitman and contract killer. That was two days before the murder of John Bickerstaffe.

A hunt for the hitman was under way, but he had so far not been located.

Superintendent Tucker checked the immaculate cut of his uniform, ran his comb for the last time through his silvering but still plentiful hair, and took a deep breath.

He was, as the Chief Constable had once told him after a television appearance on the North-West News, the acceptable face of the police. Elegant and calm, conveying the impression of an effortless competence to support the confidence he always exuded in public. His mission was to soothe those who sought reassurance, and to exercise a modicum of control over that most volatile of elements, public opinion.

It was an act, of course, but a good one. Public relations were an ever more important factor as the public perception of the police became more critical, and PR, as Tucker would tell any senior officer who was prepared to listen, was very much his forte. The Tucker act might have been more difficult to perform under the piercing scrutiny of Percy Peach, but Peach was at this moment safely incarcerated within the moving walls of the inter-city special speeding north from London. It was a thought which gave his chief an extra assurance as he went at midday into the room set up for his media conference.

The questions were what he had expected, and Tucker fielded them with aplomb. Indeed, he had managed to agree the lines of the television interview with the young girl presenter, who had just moved up to Granada from local radio and was considerably more nervous than he was. He now took her with an avuncular kindness through the main stages of the investigation into the murder of Father John Bickerstaffe, whom she had started by referring to as 'a much-loved local parish priest'.

His interrogator concluded with what she thought was a rather daring question as to whether the Superintendent in charge of the case thought the police were now near to an arrest. Thomas Bulstrode Tucker gave her his blandest smile. "You wouldn't expect me to answer that, Sally, would you? As the man directing this enquiry, I can tell you that my team has been working round the clock to bring the killer of Father Bickerstaffe to justice. We have turned up a lot of interesting information. Without wishing to appear sanguine, I can tell you that I am very happy with the progress of our work."

Tucker then sat back in his seat and contrived to look very sanguine indeed, while Sally Etherington said, "That is good for the public to hear. It seems that it won't be too long before the man who perpetrated this murder will be under lock and key."

"Or the woman. In these enlightened times, we mustn't let any question of gender cloud our sights. I'm sure that those excellent female officers who are employed on my

190

team would wish me to say that." Tucker gave the camera what he considered his most winning smile as the videotape ceased rolling.

The crime reporters at this media conference were rather less accommodating than the television presenter, but Tucker handled them with practised emollience, avoiding the confrontations which DI Peach would have relished with these hardened and cynical professionals. They were naturally interested in the involvement of a local MP, and most of the questions were aimed at establishing the place in the enquiry of Charles Courcey. Alf Houldsworth, the reporter on the local *Evening Dispatch*, hinted mischievously that Tucker had personal acquaintance with the disgraced MP, through what he called 'a social organisation with a national network'.

Tucker ignored this reference to his Masonic activities and said stiffly, "I had spoken to Mr Courcey a few times on previous occasions, yes. You would expect that a high-profile MP and a senior policeman concerned with what was going on in this part of Lancashire would come into occasional contact."

Houldsworth yawned ostentatiously during this bromide, then said, "I understand your former friend has now been charged with serious offences against children under the Child Pornography Acts."

"I believe your information is correct. The matter is not a local one. Mr Courcey, who has never been a personal friend of mine, is under arrest in London. Charges of the sort you described have already been formally laid or are pending, but they are not of course the concern of the Brunton police."

"But I understand that there is some possibility that the late MP for the Hodder Valley is also involved in the investigations you are conducting into the murder of Father Bickerstaffe.

That would be your concern, wouldn't it, Superintendent Tucker?"

Tucker couldn't believe his luck. "It would indeed, Mr . . . Mr Houldsworth, isn't it? And I can tell you that I yesterday despatched two of my senior officers to London to interview Charles Courcey in that connection." He glanced dramatically at his watch. "In fact, they should be speaking to Mr Courcey in Wormwood Scrubs Prison at this very moment." It wasn't strictly true: Peach and Blake should have concluded their enquiries some time ago and be well on the way back to Brunton by now. But he didn't see why he should let a mere fact get in the way of a fine phrase; after all, the journalists he was addressing never did that.

His statement had the desired effect. There was a buzz of interest even among these professional cynics, as they saw their column inches expanding and visualised their headlines. Tucker spent the rest of the conference emphasising that however damning and regrettable were the charges facing Charles Courcey in connection with paedophilia, there was as yet nothing tangible to link him directly with the death of Bickerstaffe. The former MP for the Hodder Valley was merely one of a number of people being investigated – his audience must surely understand that he couldn't identify these other individuals.

Alf Houldsworth attempted to restore his lost status in the journalistic tribe. "You mean you haven't a clue yet who killed our local priest?" he asked cynically.

An irritated Thomas Bulstrode Tucker crossed his meta-phorical fingers and determined to wrap up the briefing on a positive note. "On the contrary, our enquiries are now well advanced. I shall be surprised if I do not have an arrest to report to you in the next few days."

He stood up, his panache restored. He would have been less pleased with himself had he known he was repeating exactly the sentiment which had been voiced to Courcey earlier that morning by his *bête noire*, Percy Peach. For Peach was a man with whom Superintendent Tucker very rarely chose to agree.

The door of the house in Primrose Bank opened before he could use his key. Tony Reilly glanced back at a street which was reassuringly deserted beneath the dim lighting before he moved into the little terraced house.

He smiled at her and said, "There's no need for all this cloak-and-dagger stuff, you know. Covering our traces and leaving it until after dark until I come."

"You can't be too careful with the Social. Nosy lot of buggers, they are, and there's folk round here as would be only too pleased to tell them I've got a man coming into the house." Kate Maxted shut the front door firmly behind him as they went into the brightly lit living room at the front of the house and sat down.

Yet both of them knew that it wasn't the Social Services snoopers who were Kate's concern. It was their involvement in an altogether grander sort of crime that made them cautious. She looked at the clock. Half-past eight. Another day almost over, with nothing more to disturb them. No news must be good news, in these circumstances. She said, "They still haven't made any contact with you, have they, the police?"

"No. They came to the building site, the other day – well, one of them did. Cocky little bugger with a moustache. I kept out of the way: I have to, being on the lump. But it was Joe Cartwright he was interested in, not me. Wanted to tell him his alibi didn't hold water. Shook Joe up a bit, I can tell you."

Kate smiled. "Shook him even more when their Jason announced he was gay, I'm told." She was comforted by the thought that the police were following up other people, not them. She found herself wishing selfishly that Joe Cartwright might even be arrested. "I haven't seen this bloke Peach. He's a nasty piece of work, by all accounts. It was a woman who came to see me. She seemed quite nice."

"I know, you told me. But you need to be careful, all the same. You can't trust them, these police." He pronounced it in the Irish way, with a long 'o' in the first syllable.

She said, "Anyway, you're here now. I need you, Tony." And with that simple affirmation, they were in each other's arms, stroking each other's shoulders, soothing away the pains and the anxieties of the day.

Their comforting didn't last more than a few seconds. There came a violent knocking at the door Kate had so recently shut. The pair stared wide-eyed at each other; a child cried out upstairs. Kate shouted at the blank panels of the door, "Who is it?"

"It's the police, Mrs Maxted," said the muffled voice of Lucy Blake. "We need to talk to you some more."

Tony Reilly looked for a moment at Kate, then went without a word from either of them into the big kitchen which was the only other room on the ground floor and shut the door behind him.

Kate had scarcely opened the door to the street than Peach was in the room. Lucy Blake followed him more quietly, with a glance at Kate that was almost apologetic. Peach looked round the brightly lit room, taking in the cleanliness among the sparse furnishings, the battered three piece suite, the ancient television set, the school photographs of the children. Nothing stolen here: nothing good enough for that. He walked over to the door to the kitchen and threw it open. "Better come in here and join us, Tony. I've had a long day and I'm too tired for parlour games."

The big Irishman came like a shamefaced child into the room, stood confronting the Detective Inspector, who was six inches shorter than him but just as muscular. He made no move, but it was clear that he was controlling a natural instinct to hit Peach, and equally clear that Peach was going to do nothing to conciliate him.

Kate Maxted said desperately, "Shall we sit down to discuss whatever it is you want to talk about? It doesn't cost any extra to sit, you know." Her brittle laugh rang round the small room, and the four of them sat down almost in unison, watching each other as carefully as if it was a necessary stage move they were trying out for the first time. Kate said to Lucy Blake, "I thought I'd told you everything you needed when you called on Friday."

Percy gave her the smile of a lion who has cornered a very tender goat. "You didn't really think that though, did you, love? Because you'd concealed quite a lot from my colleague here. For a start, you didn't tell her that you were cohabiting with this fine figure of a man, did you?"

Reilly clenched his huge fists, pressing them against his thighs. "That's between me and Kate, that is. Or between me and the husband that's deserted her and his children and never sent her a penny of maintenance."

"Or between you and the Social Services claims department," said Percy calmly. "But I'm not here to save the taxpayers' money, Tony me boy. I'm not even interested in your working on the lump for Tommy Conlon, even though we both know you're breaking the law there. We've got bigger fish to fry, haven't we?"

Reilly glared at him for a moment before he said un-convincingly, "I don't know what you mean."

"Oh, but I think you do, Tony. Murder. The asphyxiation by means of a wire round his neck of Father John Bickerstaffe, parish priest of the Sacred Heart Church and sometime minister to you and the lovely lady beside you. Garrotting, if you prefer the technical term."

"I didn't kill him."

"No? Then why be ashamed to reveal your relationship with Mrs Maxted? Why skulk away and hide like a guilty thing when we come here tonight? Conduct of a guilty man, I'd say that is. And I have considerable experience in these matters, you see. So you're going to have to work hard to convince me, Tony."

"It's the Social, isn't it? Kate and I are serious about each other. This woman's the best thing that's happened to me in twenty years. But until I have a regular job and we can shack up together properly, we can't afford for them to know. There's four children to think about, you know."

"I know there are, Tony. I've been giving some thought to those children, you see. And particularly the eldest one, Wayne. The one who was assaulted by Bickerstaffe."

Kate Maxted came in before her lover could speak. "We've got over that now. And in any case, it was nothing to do with Tony."

Peach rounded on the woman, his face full of an earnest seriousness, as if it was important to him that he should convince her. "Really, Mrs Maxted? I'm afraid I would have to dispute both of those things. You seemed quite furious about what Bickerstaffe had done to your son when DS Blake here spoke to you on Friday." He looked up at the ceiling, appearing to call up a quotation he had memorised carefully before he left the station. "As far as I'm aware you said, 'Father Fucking Bickerstaffe, the Flashing Friar. I just wish he'd flashed at me, that's all. I'd have cut it off for him!' Hardly sounds like a woman full of Christian forgiveness, does it? And as for it being nothing to do with loverboy here, he's just told us how serious he is about you and your kids. Your hurt would be his hurt, I'd say, wouldn't you? And very nice too, for you to have some support in an uncaring world. But it does seem to argue that I can't leave either of you out of the frame for the killing of the man who abused Wayne, doesn't it?"

Reilly said, "Kate had nothing to do with killing that bloody priest, and you can't pin it on her!"

"I don't want to pin anything on her, Tony. Strange as it might seem to you, I'd like to eliminate the pair of you, if possible. It would make my job easier, and believe me after a long day that's one of the few things that appeals to me. But you aren't making it easy for us, either of you. A woman who conceals a lover and a man who is trying to conceal a history of violence."

Reilly sat bolt upright, and it seemed for an instant as if he would rise and challenge Peach. "You can't pretend that I'm—"

"Oh come on, Tony, I'm not pretending anything, and you must know it. When I found a man with your skills working on the lump, a skilled chippy who could turn his hand to plastering as well, I had to wonder why. So I checked your record, and there it was. Assault and GBH. Nearly killed a man, the last time. Four years in Walton Jail, Liverpool. Might have been less, if you hadn't hit a warder and lost your remission. Quite a man with your fists, aren't you, Tony? So perhaps also with a length of wire, I thought to myself, when I'd finished reading your record. Especially when he wants to impress

197

the woman he loves, I said to myself. Now I'm saying it to you!"

The two men had risen during this last speech of Peach's. They stood confronting each another now, not more than a foot apart, looking into each other's faces and breathing heavily, like prize fighters waiting for the bell. Lucy thought Reilly was going to hit Peach, and at that moment she would scarcely have blamed him.

But miraculously, the Irishman's control held. After a few seconds, he turned abruptly away from his opponent and said harshly to the wall, "I didn't kill yer man. I haven't hit anyone since I met Kate. And I've made her a promise: I won't." He turned back to face the Inspector. "Not even you, Peach."

Percy did not move. He confronted his man steadily for a moment longer, then said abruptly, "Where were you between five p.m. and eight p.m. on the twentieth of August, Tony Reilly?"

"That's when he was killed, isn't it?"

"It is. Where were you?"

"I finished work at Tommy Conlon's site at five. Perhaps just before that, if I'd hodded enough bricks for the brickies to start on in the morning."

"Pity. Your mates could have vouched for you if you'd been working later. Where were you after that, then? If you say in a pub on your own, I might find it difficult to believe you."

With the facts as they stated them, either Kate Maxted or Tony Reilly or both might well have been out near Bolton-by-Bowland at the time when Bickerstaffe was killed. Reilly glanced down at Kate, who was still sitting white-faced on the sofa below him. She gave him a quick nod of encouragement and he said, "I was here, with Kate."

There was a pause before Lucy Blake said quietly, "That's

not what Kate told me on Friday. She said she was here on her own. That she watched a video of *The Piano* while Wayne was playing cricket and her mother had the other kids for tea."

Kate Maxted said, equally quietly, "I wasn't telling you the truth. Well I was, except that I wasn't on my own. Tony came here soon after five and we were together for the next three hours or so."

There was a long pause. Kate's statement that her man had been with her at home might be worth no more than a wife's assurance that her husband had been with her at the time a crime was committed. It might also be as difficult to disprove. Eventually Peach said, "Have either of you anything to add to this; any further changes to make in your stories?"

Both of them shook their heads. Peach said to Lucy, "It's worth about as much as a wife's statement of support for a husband, I suppose." All four of the people in the room knew that that meant absolutely nothing, and he left the thought hanging in the air.

Sixteen

Superintendent Tucker looked at DI Peach across his huge desk with unusual smugness.

"Well, the rest of us got on with the work whilst you and Detective Sergeant Blake were frittering away the overtime budget in London," he said. Twenty hours after the conclusion of his media conference, he was still basking in the comfortable feeling of success it had brought him.

"Yes, sir. It was a consolation to us in our lonely night in the metropolis to know that the investigation was being carried forward with such verve and pace here. Have you actually made an arrest, or is that to happen this morning?"

Tucker's air of bonhomie slid to the floor and scurried away beneath his filing cabinets. "I didn't say the case had been concluded in your absence, Peach. Nothing like that. Just that the necessary work was being carried forward energetically."

"Energetically. Yes, sir. I see. Perhaps you could just bring me up to date with how things have moved in the forty-two hours since I left here on Tuesday afternoon. I haven't had a chance to talk to the team yet. I came straight up here to get the latest from the man in charge."

Tucker's flapping hands looked like the wings of a stricken pheasant above the leather of his immaculate desk. "I didn't say there been any great progress, did I? I've been busy with the things you never pay any heed to, Peach. The things you just expect to take care of themselves."

"Yes, sir. I suppose that's true. I suppose I just assume that if we catch the criminals the public will think we're doing our job. Silly of me, really."

"Absurdly over-simplistic." Tucker, unaware of any irony in Peach's view, repeated a phrase he had made into one of his clichés, then lurched into another one. "For the twenty-first century, I mean. It's time you took more notice of the world at large. While you were away, I conducted a most successful media conference. Television, the national dailies, the locals, they were all there. And I think I can say with all modesty that I gave a most telling performance."

"Yes, sir. With all modesty, I see, sir. I heard about it last night, sir, as a matter of fact. From Alf Houldsworth."

Tucker's face clouded. The local rag's sceptic was the last man he would have chosen to relate the story of his success. "Houldsworth asked one or two questions himself, in his usual cynical way. I was rather pleased with the way I answered them. I trust he was duly impressed by the conference?"

"He said you were your usual self, sir. He'd had rather too much to drink at the time, but I suppose that means that he was impressed."

Tucker was foolish enough in his vanity to chance his luck. "Didn't he say anything more specific?"

Peach fixed his frowning focus upon the ceiling in the intensity of his concentration. "I really can't recall his exact words, sir. There was some reference I didn't understand to a fart flying round a vacuum, but I couldn't really be more specific. It was nearly closing time and Houldsworth was far gone, as I said."

Tucker's face was thunderous, but he could not catch the eye

201

of his man; Peach's gaze remained obstinately upon the ceiling. "Yes, well, I'm surprised you have time to spend drinking with such people, in the middle of an investigation."

"Oh, I thought we were almost at the end of the investigation, sir. And I'd just been to see a suspect, you see." Peach dropped into his intoning voice, as if he were reading from a notebook or a file. "Second visit to Mrs Kate Maxted at eight thirty-five on the night of Wednesday, ninth of September. Concluded at nine o-four. Following upon interview at Wormwood Scrubs Prison in London with Charles Courcey from nine o-seven to nine thirty-eight on the morning of the same day."

"Yes, all right, you had a long day, Peach. There's no need to remind me of that. I expect my officers to work long days, when there's been a murder."

"Yes, sir. No objection to that, sir. You must drive us just as hard as you drive yourself, sir, as always."

Tucker looked at his man suspiciously. Peach's eyes were back with him now, or almost. They seemed to be fixed upon that spot two inches above his head which the Inspector found perennially fascinating. The Superintendent said cautiously, "What did Charles Courcey have to say for himself?"

"Not very much, sir, as far as our murder went. The paedophilia charges are not our concern, of course. Courcey was rambling on about being led astray by his friends in this area, sir. And being let down by people he'd helped in happier times."

The alarm bells clanged as urgently as a fire engine's in Tucker's contorted mind. "Masonic friends, you mean?"

"I couldn't say, sir. I never mentioned the Masons, as you have always told me they have no connections with these things. But now you mention it, I rather think he was talking about the Masons in North Lancashire, yes. People he'd helped up the social ladder who hadn't helped him in his hour of need, he said. That might well be the Masons, sir, I suppose."

Tucker wracked his brains furiously, trying to remember if he had canvassed Charles Courcey directly in his campaign to become Master of his Lodge. He couldn't remember; there were so many people he had spoken to, so many evenings of ingratiation over the years. "Ramblings, you said. Probably just that, from a desperate and disturbed man. And of no relevance to this case. So I don't think there would be any need to put them in your report."

For seconds which seemed to the agonised Tucker to stretch into minutes, Peach gave the issue his consideration. Then he said, "No, sir, I suppose not." It wouldn't be difficult to leave out things which had never occurred, after all.

Tucker tried to control his sigh of relief. "So your visit to London was rather a waste of time, was it?"

"Well, sir, it provided valuable experience for DS Blake." And for Percy Peach as well, if you did but know it, sir. Took us several minutes to untangle the sheets yesterday morning. Percy felt a seraphic smile of recollection threatening his round face and hastily resumed his official mode. "Charles Courcey obviously didn't kill Bickerstaffe himself, sir. Wouldn't have had the bottle for it, in my opinion. But there is some evidence that he and his paedophile chums employed a hitman to do the job."

"Some evidence? Really, Peach, you should know by now that you need more than vague phrases like that to convince an old hand like me. Unless you can offer me something more tangible than—"

"I can, sir. A payment was made two days before the murder to a known hitman. Name of Tucker."

Percy kept his face perfectly straight on the name; he had

practised the feat for some minutes before he came up to his chief's room.

"Tucker?"

"Tucker, sir." Then, as if the name had only this minute struck a chord, Percy's face lit up with a wonderful thought. "I say sir, the man's not a relation of yours, is he? Every family has its black sheep, but this would really be a turn-up for the books. I can imagine what the journalistic crowd would make of this, and—"

"The man is *not* a relation of mine, Peach! Get that into your thick skull! If Tucker is indeed his name." The Superintendent peered with dark suspicion at Peach across the big desk.

"Oh it is, sir. Really it is. Of course, it might be an adopted name, with a man like that. Criminals often choose to adopt the names of celebrities, apparently." Peach was studying the spot two inches above his chief's head again, with his face cleared of all expression.

"Has this man – this Tucker – been arrested?"

"Unfortunately not, sir. He's gone to earth. I doubt whether he's even in the country, if he did it."

"How much was he paid?"

"Five thousand pounds, sir." Peach waited with blank features to see if Tucker registered what he had registered when he heard that, but his chief made no comment. You're as daft and out of touch as I always thought you were, Tommy Bloody Tucker, thought Percy. And it's not up to me to dispel the black clouds of your ignorance. Superintendent.

"This contract killer will be our man," said Tucker decisively. He waved Peach from his presence. "I may have to contact Interpol presently," he said airily.

It was morning break-time at the Sacred Heart RC Primary

School, Headmistress Mrs H. MacMullen, BA. Percy Peach studied the green board with the gold lettering by the school gate, watched the raucous mass of young humanity in the playground for a moment, then moved on impulse into the cool silence of the church beside the school.

Percy had been reared as a Catholic boy. Thirty years ago, when he had been as noisy and unthinking as those noisy seven-year-olds he had watched for a moment in the playground, he had had the blind certainty in his God that only a child of that age can possess. He had lost his belief long ago, but the habits bred in the very young die hardest of all, and he found himself genuflecting before the altar in the empty church. He knelt for a moment, bending his stubborn knees in prayer to the God who just might after all be there. It was just as well to play safe with these things, he told his more cynical self, as it tried to reassert itself.

He even asked the Almighty to be merciful to the person or persons he would eventually arrest for the murder of Father John Bickerstaffe, late priest of this parish. He would never confess to anyone that he had done any such thing, not even to Lucy Blake, though he felt very close to her now. What he felt and what he did in this church were entirely between him and this God who almost certainly didn't exist.

Percy wandered to the back of the deserted church, inspected the rotas for cleaning, for shutting the church, for serving Mass. He noted the reappearance on this week's list of servers of the name of Jamie Hanlon. There was no sign of Jason Cartwright, or Thomas Kennedy, or Wayne Maxted. But there was nothing significant in that: they hadn't been regular servers at Mass before they were assaulted by Bickerstaffe, so they were hardly likely to appear on the lists of servers with the new priest. Percy ignored the stoup of holy water by the door as he left the church: you had to draw the line somewhere.

He wandered round the side of the deserted church and knocked at the door of the presbytery. Martha Hargreaves was expecting him, had seen him go into the church and approved. There is more joy in heaven over the return of one repentant sinner than . . . Martha couldn't remember the rest, but it meant there was always hope, even for a policeman.

She had coffee waiting for him and they chatted surprisingly easily across the cups, this old-fashioned, pious spinster and this dapper taker of felons. He took her through her description of the man who had called at the presbytery to try to retrieve Charles Courcey's letter to Bickerstaffe, but she could not be any more precise than she had already been to the uniformed constable five days earlier. "It was dark and he was muffled to the eyes. And I sent him packing pretty quickly. I couldn't see much, except that he was tall and dark and fairly young. Is it important?"

"Probably not," said Percy. This certainly wasn't the hitman the paedophiles had commissioned to kill Bickerstaffe; probably no more than a minor bit of muscle retained to frighten less resolute citizens than Martha Hargreaves. Time to change the subject. "Used to serve Mass myself, in the old days," said Percy, stretching his short legs out before him and biting into a home-made ginger biscuit.

"Those experiences are always with you, until the day you die," said Martha. "Or so they tell me. I never got further than cleaning the brasses, myself." Was there a hint of resentment at the female lot there, even from this most loyal and traditional of church servants?

"Notice young Jamie Hanlon's back on the roster."

She looked at him suspiciously, but he was smiling and

relaxed, looking past her to the picture of Saint Theresa on the wall behind her. "Aye. He's had a talk with the new priest, Father Brown, and told him he wanted to come back."

"Good thing, I expect. I notice you even have a rota for shutting the church up at night, nowadays. Pity it's necessary, but I'm afraid it is."

"Expect the police are too busy with other things to protect churches." Martha sniffed disgustedly.

"Afraid that's so," said Percy, not at all put out. "Murders, for instance."

"And other things. It's a nasty world. Not like the one I was brought up in. Even people who call themselves Catholics don't go to church every Sunday, nowadays." She offered it as the ultimate evidence of declining standards, and Percy was secretly inclined to agree with her.

"I see the Hanlons are on the roster. Keith Hanlon was supposed to lock up the church on the night of the twentieth of August, I noticed."

"The night when Father was killed." The old eyes stared at him steadily, letting him know that she read her papers and listened to her television like younger people, that she was aware of what he was about.

"Yes, we believe it was that night. I don't suppose you know if the rota was observed that night, or whether there was any switch? I know you close the church up yourself sometimes, when someone can't take their turn."

Martha studied him with her head a little on one side, then allowed herself a small, rather tired smile. "The roster was observed, as you call it, on the night of the twentieth. Pat Hanlon shut up the church at seven o'clock. I popped out myself to check that the church was safe – having no priest in residence, you see. I put my head out just before *The*

Archers came on, and I saw Pat Hanlon leaving. Does that disappoint you?"

"Not at all. It's a bit of information, that's all. It's my job to gather information, you know. You must be glad to see things getting back to normal, to have a priest in the house again. I expect the parishioners are, too. The Cartwrights are back at the Sacred Heart, are they?"

Martha looked at him keenly, then offered him the plate of her gingernuts, as if that confirmed her approval. "They've never been away. They're always at Sunday Mass – they came even when we were being serviced by the priests from St Mary's."

"And the Kennedy boys? Are they back?"

"No. The father's never been, but the boys came regularly on Sundays when Father Bickerstaffe was here. I haven't seen them since then. They might be going down to St Mary's, of course."

But you don't think they are, any more than I do, thought Percy. He imagined the look of triumph on the ageing face of David Kennedy when he saw his boys ceasing their attendance at the church he hated. "What about Kate Maxted?"

"She's at Mass and Communion regularly enough on Sundays, and her children with her. And so's your man Reilly."

"You know about that?"

Martha smiled a smile of infinite experience. "Of course I know. I don't gossip, but they don't trouble to disguise it. Father Bickerstaffe knew, and he was hoping they'd get together properly. Said it would be the making of Tony Reilly. He's the kind of old-fashioned Irish Catholic who smashes faces in on Saturday nights and is there at the Communion rail on Sunday mornings, Father said. But there's a good man underneath. And Kate Maxted deserves a good man.

She had a rotten husband, but she's devoted to her children, is Kate."

They talked a little longer, as Peach prolonged the fiction both of them shared that this was a social visit. He found himself enjoying her company. When you dealt for so much of your time with villains and their associates, it was tempting to linger with someone as genuine as Martha Hargreaves.

In the murder room set up at Brunton CID, Peach did at the end of that Thursday afternoon what the Superintendent in charge of the case should have been doing. He reviewed the latest evidence from the extensive team assigned to a murder investigation.

"What's Tommy Bloody Tucker doing?" he asked Lucy Blake, who had been bringing the computer files up to date whilst he visited the presbytery at the Sacred Heart and then checked the latest findings on their suspects.

"Very little, apart from panicking. He's cut out all overtime here until his namesake the contract killer is located. He's put out a nationwide alert for Francis Ward Tucker, on suspicion of murder."

"Fat lot of good that will do! It's one of the skills of the contract killer to disappear completely when they're most sought by people like us. Anyway, he didn't kill John Bickerstaffe."

"Courcey seemed to think he might have."

"Courcey knows bugger all about murder! No more than Tommy Bloody Tucker, our esteemed leader and superprat."

"Why are you so certain of that?"

"Because of the price, my chicken! Five grand isn't the price for a murder. Not from a professional killer like Francis Tucker. Not when he knows the people hiring him can call on the money of Charles Courcey and others."

"So how do you explain the five thousand pounds?"

"A down payment. Five thousand at the outset, to set things in hand, another ten, perhaps fifteen thousand when the killing is successfully achieved. There's no evidence that this second and larger sum was ever paid: it's been checked and re-checked. This man got his five thousand, was setting up the killing in his own time. Only someone stepped in and did his job for him. Deprived him of the final fee, but also of any risk. Five thousand quid for nix. Make yourself scarce for a while, in case news of the down-payment leaks out and the boys in blue come looking for you."

Lucy said dully, "I didn't know the price of a killing."

"It's not fixed, and you won't find it in any of the manuals. You look at what's happened recently, at the rare occasions when a professional contract-killer is brought to book. Birmingham, last year. I wouldn't expect you to know. I wouldn't expect Tommy Bloody Tucker to know, but he damn well *should*!" For an instant, Peach's real resentment and frustration burst out.

"So what next?" said Lucy Blake.

Peach was on his feet. "Time for a bit of bluff," he said decisively. "It's my guess the people who did this haven't the heart for deception, for brazening it out. Let's go!"

Seventeen

The clouds had dropped in low over the narrow brick streets of the old cotton town, emphasising the rapidly shortening September days, bringing in a very early twilight, reminding everyone that autumn was at hand.

For Percy Peach, who had been a cricketer of note in the Lancashire League until two years ago, it was sad to see that the boys on the spare land they passed had abandoned the summer game and were chasing a football in their shrill groups; another cricket season was over. Lucy Blake was driving the police Mondeo; glancing sideways at her companion, she was surprised to see how grim he looked, his lips set in a thin line, his forehead furrowed with a frown. Usually when they were near to an arrest he was exhilarated, driven forward by the lust of the hunter near his prey, that essential quality of all successful CID officers.

He gave her terse directions, no more. Eventually she risked a quick, "Why so grim?"

He glanced at her for the first time, affording her a quick smile, a gratified recognition that she should catch his mood so quickly.

"This job gets to you, sometimes. I should be glad we're wrapping this one up. And of course I am – that's what the job's about. I just wish it could have had a different outcome, this time."

It was the first time in years he had been prepared to declare so much of himself, to reveal a crack in the facade of Percy Peach, clear-headed, ruthless thief-taker and hardman of Brunton CID. He found his admission more of a relief than he would ever have expected, so much so that he wanted to enlarge upon it. "There are kids involved. Kids who are going to lose good parents."

"You know the answer to that. We solve crimes; we don't play God. We pin down the criminals: it's up to the courts to take account of the circumstances which surround a crime. You've told me that often enough."

He twitched a little, partly with his impatience at the familiar phrases, partly with his resentment that he should find this weakness in himself. "I know all that. Perhaps in this case I'll be hoping for once that the court listens to the trick-cyclists. I don't know how I'd have reacted myself if I'd had a son abused, do I?"

"No. None of us knows what we'd have done." She wondered for a moment if she would ever have a son by this still surprising man beside her, then steered herself away from such dangerous ground. "Fortunately, we don't have to speculate. We may bring people to justice, but what form that justice takes has nothing to do with us."

"No. You're right, of course – it's the only way we can operate. But we see enough of that justice to see how flawed it can sometimes be. I hope these kids don't end up with Social Services."

They were almost at the house, and she said no more. And Percy Peach, like a man donning the mask of brisk efficiency, was his normal dynamic and aggressive self by the time he rang the bell by the door of the cramped modern detached house.

They could hear the sound of children's voices from behind the building, but these modern houses were built so close to each other that it was not clear whether the shrill sounds came from the rear garden of this house or from one of its neighbours. The white-faced woman who answered the door led them into the lounge of the house and they saw with relief that the garden was deserted. Peach took in the tidy, well-worn furnishings, the empty garden, the soundless house, all without taking his eyes from the woman who had led them here. He sat down with Lucy Blake as she gestured towards one of the room's twin sofas.

Only then did he say, "You seem almost as if you were expecting us, Mrs Hanlon."

"I wasn't. I don't know what you—"

"Children out, are they?"

"Yes. They're with their cousins. They're having tea at my sister's house. She's like a second mother to them – even more so since that – that trouble Jamie had."

"I'm glad to hear that."

"They'll be in presently, if you want to—"

"No need for that, Mrs Hanlon. Your husband's here though, is he?"

She looked towards the door, where her husband had appeared without a sound, as if responding to a stage cue. "I heard the voices," he said. He spoke almost apologetically, thought Lucy Blake. Keith Hanlon came into the room, took his wife's hand, and pulled her gently to sit beside him on the sofa, directly facing the two CID officers. There was a pause. He glanced down the garden towards the black ashes of his bonfire, invisible in the gathering gloom to all save him, before he said, "What can we do to help you, Inspector Peach? I thought we'd said all we had to say to each other when you came here on Saturday."

"If you really want to be helpful, you could tell us exactly how you killed Father John Bickerstaffe," said Peach quietly.

He might have been asking for directions to a destination, not accusing a man of the gravest crime of all. Kevin Hanlon did not react physically, save to put his hand on the wrist of the wife who had flinched so palpably at his side. He said with a forced calmness, "You'd better have good reasons for saying that."

He hadn't denied it, and neither had she, Percy noticed. Time to implement the bluff, to make a few bricks out of precious little straw. "What happened to Jamie appeared to have hit you hardest of all the parents involved. That doesn't make you murderers, of course. But you had your story of where you both were at the time of the murder very well rehearsed: you gave us the details of what you were supposed to have been doing between five and seven thirty on Thursday the twentieth of August as though you had been over it many times before you spoke to us."

Hanlon looked down at his hand, which had slid down now to cover his wife's, thinking furiously, feeling his way into speech before she could say anything revealing. "I'm prepared to admit that we had talked about that before you came here on Saturday. But it doesn't mean we killed the man who had assaulted our son. We knew he'd been murdered: it's only natural that we should have anticipated your questions, that we should have thought carefully about exactly what we were doing at the time he was killed."

"Except of course that if you were innocent you shouldn't have known what time the victim died," said Peach calmly.

214

"The news of Bickerstaffe's murder had been made public by the time we spoke to you. The time had still not been revealed. Yet you admitted just now that you discussed your alibis for that time before we came to see you."

Keith Hanlon sat very still on the sofa, feeling the rigidity of his wife beside him, willing her not to speak, not even to look up into his face. Even a look could be fatal now, he felt. He tried hard to sound calm as he said, "You'll have to do better than that, Inspector Peach. I told you, even the innocent can examine what they were doing at any particular time."

"And even the guilty can agree their stories, Mr Hanlon. Can make up a lie and then test each other to see that their stories tally, that they are giving each other an alibi for a particular time, a time they should not have known was important but somehow did. It always seemed that this wasn't an individual crime, that whoever tightened that wire round Bickerstaffe's neck had a partner who had helped him to set it up and provided him with an alibi for the time of the killing."

Pat looked up into her husband's face sharply on the phrase about the wire round the victim's neck, and Peach knew in that moment that she had never until then known the exact details of the garrotting of the man who had abused her son. Keith had protected her from that, just as now he tried to protect both of them by pressing his hand down warningly on top of hers.

Keith was afraid of what she might say, but when she spoke at last it was an attempt to defend him. "We were here that night," she said in a monotone. "Here at seven o'clock on that night. And I can prove it. It was our turn to shut up the church. The Sacred Heart. We still did it, you know, even after – after what Father did to Jamie. You can look at the roster for church security if you don't—"

"*You* were here on that night, Mrs Hanlon. But your husband wasn't. Not at seven o'clock. Your husband's name was on the roster, but it was you who shut the church. You took his place, because he wasn't back home at that time."

She could have denied it. She could have given him lots of reasons for the change other than her husband's absence. He would have known they were false, but he could not have disproved them. But she was a naturally truthful woman, with none of the resources of the habitual deceiver. She looked at Peach for a moment in horrified silence, then her resolve cracked. "That man deserved it!" she shouted. "He abused our boy! Our Jamie, who never hurt a fly!"

Then, suddenly, her arms were round her husband and she was in tears. It was Keith Hanlon who had to conclude the bizarre ritual of confession. "Pat phoned him the night before and arranged that she would meet him in a ruined barn we knew, just outside Bolton-by-Bowland that Thursday evening. I waited in the barn until he came and then jumped him from behind. It was easy – he was only expecting Pat, you see. I hit him over the head with a cricket stump, before he even saw me. I didn't give him the chance to speak. If he had spoken, had argued with me, had asked for mercy, I wouldn't have been able to do it."

At this thought, Pat Hanlon was wracked by a renewed bout of sobbing; he pressed her head against his chest and stroked it gently, whispering wordless comfortings, as a mother might do to a child. Then he spoke again to the two faces opposite him. "He was unconscious, after I hit him. I tightened the wire around his neck before he could come round and look at me."

Lucy Blake said gently, "Why did it take you so long to get home after you'd killed him?"

"I had to hide the body, didn't I? That's why we'd arranged

216

he should meet me there. There was a wood behind the barn, with a deep ditch beside it. We'd picnicked there you see, when the children were younger, so we knew the spot well. I emptied the pockets. There was a letter there, threatening what would happen to him if he didn't keep his mouth shut about some photographs. I'm afraid I burned it with the other things." He was genuinely apologetic, as if he regretted this minor breach of the law more than the crime of murder.

Lucy nodded, then asked quietly, "What did you do with the body?"

"I put the body in the ditch, in the spot I'd selected before he came. It was a good five feet deep at that point, and overgrown – there was no water in it at that time. If it hadn't been for that torrential downpour on the Bank Holiday Monday, it could have been undiscovered for years."

Act of God, they call that, thought Peach. He didn't voice the thought to these devastatingly pious people. Instead, he radioed for assistance as Lucy Blake uttered the formal words of arrest over the couple, still clasped in each other's arms but now both weeping. The uniformed men who arrived looked very young, even to Peach's eyes. They took the unresisting couple out to the car. "No need for the cuffs," said Peach quietly as they went.

Pat Hanlon turned her face back to him at the door. "Father Bickerstaffe should never have done that, not to our boy. He didn't deserve to live. And him a priest. Bringing disgrace to Holy Mother Church." She sounded as if she still thought that might be a bigger sin than the assault itself.

Lucy Blake stayed behind to break the news of what had happened to the children. She made a swift phone call to the children's aunt, then set off to walk the half-mile to her house, rehearsing the wording of her dreadful news as she went.

Peach went with the Hanlons to prepare the formal charges at the station. They seemed almost peaceful, quieter now with the relief of confession, that relief which their religion had afforded them all their lives. As if she divined Peach's thoughts, Pat Hanlon turned to her husband in the back of the police vehicle and said, "We'll be able to go to Confession now, and receive absolution from our sins, won't we, Keith?"

Her husband nodded, unable to speak, pressing his hand upon her arm to try to silence her. But she said contentedly to Peach in the front seat of the car, "They'll allow us a visit from a priest in prison, won't they?"